MW01045804

Delicate Scars

By

Alta Hensley

Dedication

To my sweet Ava and Kenna.
Everything I do is for you.
And to Mr. Hensley…my dream maker.

Alta Hensley

Chapter 1

Love At First Fucking Sight

Quinn

Is it possible to pick that one defining moment in life that fucked you up? I think it is fair to say that everyone in the world is messed up one way or the other. But can everyone look back on their life and pinpoint the exact minute it happened? I used to believe I wasn't fucked up. I had absolutely no reason to be. I was actually one of the few people who could say I had a good childhood. Middle income family, parents who stayed married, average upbringing. Nothing there to fuck me up.

Maybe I could say I was fucked up by Anthony Cruz when he tried to take my virginity at the age of fifteen, but it wasn't like rape or anything. I thought I was ready but it still felt like he was taking it rather than me giving it. So, I screamed no, and luckily for me, he stopped. However, other than the fact that he lied and told everyone we had hot and wild sex, then dumped me right afterwards, I still wouldn't say he fucked me up.

My life was fairly easy growing up. I wouldn't exactly say I was spoiled, but I never had to struggle. My parents paid for my car when I was sixteen, paid for my entire college education so I never had to get some lame part time job, and even helped pay my bills now so I could follow my dream of becoming a novelist.

My sister had died recently, and although it ripped my soul out of my body and shredded my heart into a million pieces, I survived. It didn't change the core of who I was, nor put me in the fucked up category. I was able to move on just like every other person in the world who has lost a loved one. I went on one day at a time. But the truth of the matter was life simply wasn't a struggle for me. Call me one of the lucky ones, I guess.

I wasn't fucked up…

Until I met *him*.

Axel Rye.

Yes.

He fucked me up.

He *really* fucked me up.

The deafening club music pulsated through my body, the bass pounding at my ears like a hammer. I made a mental note to try to describe the sensation when I wrote my book. One more thing to add to my ever-growing list of story notes. I wanted my readers to understand the power the music possessed. I wanted to somehow successfully describe how the sound waves actually woke every nerve in your body and caused each one to vibrate from your head to your toes. I wanted to explain in detail how each thump of the bass made your entire core hum in excitement. Recounting this club would definitely be a challenge. How could you possibly express the inside of a nightclub without sounding like a washed-up poet?

I took off my apron at the end of my shift, desperate for a break. Standing on my feet for so many hours was a lot harder than I thought it would be. Bartending was no joke, and after working the job for one night, I felt bad for not tipping all my bartenders in the past way better than I did. My feet were killing me and that was with me wearing black ballet-slipper-like shoes, unlike all the five-inch heels the other women in the club wore. How they stood and balanced on the spikes, let alone danced, amazed me.

The club was hot, sticky, crowded, and I really wanted to get some fresh air and maybe a small moment of silence. I scanned the room, looking for my friend Felicity again. She had promised to meet me at the club before my shift ended and at least be a familiar face amongst the crowd of complete strangers.

The girl could socialize her way through anything. Selfish as fuck sometimes, but she had been my friend since sixth grade, and we just meshed somehow. She was wild; I was not. She was fun, while I bored even myself sometimes. She had helped me land this job, a job completely out of my element, bartending at one of the most popular clubs in Los Angeles. Felicity had also offered me a place to stay while I did the research needed to write my book on the seedy life of nightclubs, drugs, and all the glitz and glamour laced with gritty shadows. I had high hopes I'd get enough real life details to expand into a book, but didn't know how much information I could really gather. My editor Harrison—if you could really call him an editor since he only free-lanced for beginners like me and was trying to break into the publishing world himself—had thought it would be a good idea for me to completely go undercover and immerse myself in the everyday life... or nightlife, as it were. He said I lived in a suburban dollhouse and had no idea what happened beyond the key-entry gates. And unless I wanted to write a cookbook or some sugary puppy love young adult romance, I had to branch out and expand my life experiences. I agreed the investigation might make my book more genuine and complex, and I did feel as if I was trapped in the white box of boring. I also didn't want to just get the generic, canned answers from an interview. Or write about something I knew absolutely nothing about and risk the readers sensing my ignorance. I had never been a partier unless you counted the couple times I drank from a beer bong at a frat party. But for this book—especially since it would be my debut—I wanted to go deeper and really capture the heart behind it all. I wanted the truth, the feelings, the reality.

Glancing at the clock, I saw that Felicity was over an hour late. Had my friend really flaked on me? Felicity had a habit of getting "lost," but she wouldn't just forget about me, or at least I hoped not. I had counted on her for a ride back to our apartment. Not wanting to walk through the wall of sweaty bodies by myself, I decided to just stay put a little longer and wait for her. I took in some of the faces around me and wondered if I should mingle and make some friends.

Yeah, like that was really going to happen.

Being outgoing was not my strength, so I chose to sit and observe instead.

A commotion got my attention, and I turned toward the front entrance to find a crowd gathered around a group of men who had just walked in. I stiffened, the hair on the back of my neck standing on end. I swallowed the lump forming in the back of my throat, my heart leaping as I saw the man I wanted to get to know. He was the key to my success. Tall. Handsome. Tattoos in all the right places. Face hidden in darkness. The pictures I had seen, and all the media coverage I'd watched, did not do this man justice. A single picture could not capture the raw power and strength rippling through him. The control, the authority, the mystery.

Axel Rye.

I watched with interest. I'd been told this club—*Wicked*—was the place to be. I hadn't heard of it before, not until Felicity raved about the place and the people who frequented the spot like Axel Rye. He was clearly in demand by just watching all the people turn his way the minute he walked in. My new boss at the club confirmed my belief that Axel Rye was the hot ticket when he had told me to always cater to Axel and his friends' needs. Never say no to the man. I was told Axel provided something crucial to the nightclub and the partygoers—drugs.

Trying to act cool, but feeling uneasy being in the same room with a known drug dealer, I looked around for Felicity again, feeling more than a little annoyed at still having to wait. I was completely out of my element and having serious doubts I could even do this… that I even *wanted* to do this. Who was I to think I could simply immerse myself in the scene and hang out with celebrities like Axel Rye…

if you really could call him a celebrity? Although I guess in this scene he was—as fucked up as that was. Notoriety equaled fame, and Axel Rye was definitely notorious.

A deep wave of laughter erupted directly behind me, and I turned to find the same group of men I'd seen walk in just moments earlier. A flock of women surrounded them, flirting, dancing, and having a good time. Axel Rye stood in the middle of it all. He looked different than when I last saw him on television. Granted, when I watched him on TV he was in a suit and tie being escorted out of a courthouse by his team of lawyers after just being found not guilty of all drug charges. I had watched in awe when his arrogant ass hopped in a black Escalade as if he was innocent as an angel.

He was guilty.

Everyone knew it. He just had the money to buy his way out of a jail sentence. Or his rich rock star daddy did. Axel Rye was the son of the famous singer Jamison Rye, and the word "rich" wasn't a strong enough term to describe the wealth that family had. They were helicopters and yacht rich. Axel Rye—though everyone thought was cool as fuck—was nothing but a trust fund baby. He hadn't worked a real job a day in his life, so the fact he sold drugs wasn't out of need to feed his family, pay for medical bills or for any other romanticized reason. No, he simply sold drugs because he wanted to and because he could.

But God, he was fucking handsome as hell.

And he was so close I could reach out and touch him if I wanted to. I had researched the crap out of this guy, and even though he was a complete stranger, I did have an odd sense I knew him. I had stared at his face and read countless articles while brainstorming and outlining my book. As odd as it was, this man was no stranger to me.

He was laughing when our eyes met, and I almost peed my pants from the huge weight in my stomach when I realized he caught me staring at him. His laugh stopped, and the smile on his face seemed to melt away slowly. He stood there frozen, his chiseled face almost demanding to be touched. The scar near his lower lip caught my eye. For a moment, I thought he might say something, but then I heard Felicity come up behind me.

"Hey there," she said, a bit winded.

I snapped out of my groupie stare and watched as she wiggled her way to the bar and ordered a drink. "Crazy night! Sorry I'm so late."

"It's okay. I was actually hoping to leave. It's been a long night."

Acting as if she hadn't heard me, she simply stared ahead until the bartender made and delivered her her drink. She grabbed her cocktail and spun around, taking in the dancing bodies around her. Bobbing her head to the music, she instantly fit in. "You do realize, Quinn, who that was staring at you, right?"

Slightly embarrassed, I pretended to not comprehend. "No one was staring at me."

Felicity gasped. "That was Axel Rye! You two were staring at each other. The man was actually giving you the time of day. You guys had direct eye contact. I saw it!"

"No, we weren't," I lied. I could hardly breathe now because of that brief moment, but I didn't want to admit it. And the reality is that if Axel Rye was really staring at me, it was because I clearly was out of place. I was the square peg and he knew it. I was Waldo and he had simply spotted me. Nothing more.

"Look at you! Say whatever you want, but I see it. You've been here one night and you're already making headway. Leave it to you to find the most fucked up, yet sexiest man in this room. I knew you'd fit in just fine." Felicity took a large swig of her drink. "Let's go out there and show them what we got."

She grabbed me by the arm and pulled me onto the dance floor before I could object.

* * * * *

Axel

I made my way to the VIP section of the club. My head pounded as the techno music pulsated in my ringing ears. My veins still burned from the dirty heroine I shot up last night. The only good that came from that fucked up incident was I made the decision I was done with H forever. Fuck that shit. I had lost too many friends to that drug, and I definitely didn't want to be some homeless junkie, fucking whatever dealer I could for a chance to share a disease-infested needle. Things in my life were spiraling out of control enough as it was, and I didn't need to add heroine junkie to the list. No more needles.

I wasn't in the mood to be at *Wicked* or any club at all. It was the second time this week for this club, but the fourth time being out on a *request by owner*. Even the line of coke I snorted before entering the club wasn't helping my mood of feeling forced like a god damned prisoner to be there. *Request by owner* meant I got paid for even walking through the doors. Treated like fucking royalty all because I walked on the dark side and played the sick game. I only mingled, shook hands and gave false hugs to strangers because I got paid to do it.

I got paid a lot.

Unlike my father who was famous for his music, I was famous for one thing: I was a drug dealer. Always having a constant supply of good shit caused me to be in high demand at every bar, club, and trendy restaurant in town. What once used to be very secretive, behind-closed-doors, and hush-hush had recently become very visible. There was no secret I dealt. After my last arrest and the media circus around my hearing, when it came to trendy drugs for the rich, the famous, and the cool kids, I was seen as the face of it. Media took hold of the idea, and the rest spiraled out of control. Being a bad boy was hot, and I was about as bad as they got right now. It was fucking nuts.

I nodded to and acknowledged all the club-goers gazing my way. Some of the other guys I hung with were already doing shots, popping pills, snorting lines and beginning the party. I was high, but not nearly as high as they were. My entourage kept the energy to the extreme, the fun flowing, and the night alive until the wee hours. They earned every penny the nightclub paid them. Me, on the other hand... I had the charm. I had the reputation. And I had the name of Axel Rye. *Rye* was notorious. My charisma and lure worked its magic as usual tonight, although my smile was anything but genuine. The odd popularity had stopped making me uncomfortable a long time ago, especially among drunk women throwing themselves at me, but I would never get used to everyone wanting to buy drugs. The hunger in their veins made them beg for more, and they would pay whatever price I set for it. I had full control of them, like a demonic puppet master. They were all nothing but junkies in fancy clothes. I hated it.

Although it was once nice to have instant notoriety the minute I walked into a room, now I resented having to always be the life of the party. I had the looks, the right aura, the status, and everyone wanted to be a part of it. I definitely could be an arrogant asshole. But somewhere along the line, that shit got old. My life was a damn sick joke, and I had no one to blame but myself. I never knew who truly wanted to be around me for me, and who just wanted the limelight or the access to cheap or even free drugs. I learned to trust nobody. Hell... I didn't even trust myself.

Lost in my thoughts and wanting a moment for myself, I made my way towards the dance floor. I hated to dance, but I didn't really mind the music. Blocking out everyone around me, I closed my eyes and just leaned up against a pillar near the crush of swaying bodies but not among them, taking in the beat of the music. The heat of the room and the close proximity of bodies caused sweat to trickle down my back. I slightly bobbed my head to the beat, enjoying the isolation the rhythm of the bass gave me. Being the son of a rock star, I grew up to appreciate the skill of a musician. It had always disappointed my father I never followed in his footsteps. Not that the bastard ever spent a minute trying to teach me how to play the guitar or sing a note. No, he was too busy touring the world and being the famous Jamison Rye. And my mother was too busy being a socialite to even remember she had a son. I had dabbled in being a DJ, and my name alone sold out any venue I spun at. Clubs all around the world wanted me. But the truth of the matter was, I sucked at it. I couldn't compete with the DJs I actually respected and even called my friends. I was man enough to admit it just wasn't my gig. Not to mention I made a hell of a lot more money selling for an hour than I did spinning for one.

Someone brushed right past me, a little too close.

Motherfucking groupie. They were all the same. *Accidently* knocking into me. *Accidently* getting my attention. All until I gave them the time of day, and then they *purposely* became an annoying gnat I wouldn't be able to shake for the rest of the night. It always ended with them wanting to blow me for some drugs.

Blow for some blow. Story of my life.

Annoyed, I took a soothing breath when I realized the person who bumped into me was the same girl who'd caught my attention at the bar. I hadn't seen her before—not that I recognized all the chicks in every nightclub. But this one stood out to me. She seemed different. She was gorgeous, but not in the fake—I've spent two hours on my make-up and hair—type of gorgeous like most of the women in *Wicked*. No, this girl was your typical girl-next-door-type of gal, clearly lost in a dark and dank place like this.

"I'm so sorry. I didn't mean to knock into you. Did I hurt you?" By her awkward stance, and the embarrassment washing over her face, I could tell she really hadn't meant to bump into me. She couldn't even hold my gaze for more than a few moments before her gaze slid away.

"No, I'm good." I swiped at my hair that now lay limply against my forehead. I found it odd that I suddenly felt self-conscious about my appearance, but I didn't want her to think I was a sweaty junkie lowlife.

"You sure you're okay?" the girl asked again.

This time, she held my gaze, the concern showing in hers. I looked into her deep brown eyes for the first time—clear and not dilated like every other girl in the club—and my heart beat hard against my chest. The laser lights swirled behind the girl, casting her in full light one second and in a shadow the next. I smiled at her petite silhouette. Every time her face lit up, I noticed her eyes first. They were an amazing rich chocolate color, unlike anything I had ever seen. They matched perfectly with her dark brown hair that reflected all the colored lights around her. Thick, full eyelashes curved slightly at the end, providing the perfect frames for such a pair of beautiful eyes. She was a true beauty. The girl stared back at me as she stood there breathing hard.

Her brown hair was up in a loose bun, except for a few strands that lightly rested on the sides of her face and forehead. It surprised me she didn't seem fazed by my notoriety. Almost as if she didn't know who I was, which would be impossible unless she lived under a rock. You couldn't go onto social media or turn on the television and not see my face plastered all over it. She acted genuinely sorry for knocking into me. It didn't seem like she had done it intentionally, like the game so many others had played in the past. That game had gotten really old.

"I'm fine," I said, wishing I hadn't done the coke. My head spun, and the lights swirling around her weren't helping the situation. I was too high to have this conversation, but I really wanted to. But she was sober and I was not, which was always a recipe for disaster.

"Good." The girl tucked the loose hair behind her ear and turned to resume her dancing. She didn't look back or ask anything else. She seemed impatient to be on her way. I watched in fascination as she seductively moved her hips to the music.

With my heart pounding and the overpowering need to see her face again surging, to my own surprise, I tapped her on the shoulder and stammered, "So, I haven't seen you here before."

Fuck! I was too high for this shit. I was sounding like a dumb ass.

The girl turned and looked at me without responding. Maybe she hadn't heard me. I hoped her lack of words weren't just because she thought I was an idiot. Although I sounded like a fucking idiot.

"I'm Axel, what's your name?" Trying to keep my cool was as difficult as walking under water.

"Quinn Sullivan."

All I could manage was a weak smile as I allowed the most alluring name I had ever heard to descend into my soul. High or not, I liked her name. It seemed to fit her perfectly.

"Well, have a good night," Quinn said, and danced off, fading into the crowd of bodies. She was leaving me, and I really didn't have a choice but to let her.

Why did I care?

But I did.

I did care.

I reluctantly made my way back to the VIP section to join my friends as my thoughts went back to those brown eyes cloaked in black lashes. Quinn Sullivan and the enticing eyes.

Yeah, I was fucking high.

Chapter 2

Knight In Fucked Up Armor

Quinn

I danced off, concentrating on trying to be as graceful as possible as I walked back to the bar where Felicity was ordering another drink. I had a feeling Axel was still watching me, and I would die of embarrassment if I fell or stumbled. My awkward nerves were out of control. How could I almost knock the man over? Of all people, it had to be the famous, and sexy as hell Axel Rye. I should've said more to him, but I'd been at a loss for words, and thoughts. All I could do was gawk at him like a crazed fan or druggy. I was positive he thought I did it on purpose. He probably expected for me to ask to buy some drugs or take a selfie with him to show off online.

My knees had almost buckled when I realized who I had accidentally danced into. I had no business dancing. I seriously sucked ass at it, and all but appeared to be having a seizure on the dance floor. But leave it to me to dance into Axel Rye! I was so lame.

I had researched all about the great Axel Rye and his drug-dealing clan. Felicity partied at the same hot spots as they did. She desperately wanted to be let into their popular social circle. I had never really grasped everything Felicity told me about Axel and his friends. She made them out to be movie star, drop-dead gorgeous, and after seeing them in person, I would have to agree. But the truth of the matter was what they did for a living was still against the law and wrong. How everyone looked up to them, and practically treated them as Gods surprised me. They were just drug dealers, though alluring ones at that.

Axel Rye was too gorgeous for his own good. My heart thumped wildly as I tried my best not to look over my shoulder to see if he was staring at me. I really wished I weren't so attracted to that man. But how could I not be? With his messy dark, chestnut brown hair, sexy, mysterious eyes, and lean, muscular body, Axel was a walking vision. The ink of his tattoos beckoned my curiosity. Everything about him teased my senses—his looks, his raspy baritone voice, his tantalizing, sultry scent. And God help me, I was attracted to the fact that he was a bad boy. I shouldn't be, but I was fascinated by it.

Making my way back to the bar, I looked over at the VIP section where Axel sat with a large group of men and women, most covered in tattoos, piercings, trendy clothes, and looking like the hippest stylist in LA had dressed them all. Axel and his friends seemed to glide in a lingering wave toward a group of girls. They had a mysticism in their actions. In the way they moved. Almost like vampires in a dark blockbuster movie. The women waited, their eager smiles reminding me of teenyboppers at a boy band concert.

Axel wore a tight black shirt that showed off his firm arms. Tattoos marked his entire exposed skin. His black pants clung to his body as if they were designed just for him. I had never seen a more seductive smile on a man. His masculine look screamed alpha. Rough, rugged, and at the same time, handsome. The scar by his mouth had an incredible draw, giving him a lure that pulled anyone in. I watched as one of the slinky-clad women practically lunged into Axel's arms, smothering the man with her breasts, and then looked around nonchalantly to make sure everyone was watching.

"Is that Axel's girlfriend?" I asked Felicity as I leaned over to speak into her ear to be heard over the booming cadence.

Felicity glanced over to where the woman hung off Axel and shook her head. "Only in her wildest dreams. That's Jillian, one of the coke head sluts who clings to that group. She relentlessly tries to convince anyone who will listen that the two of them are a couple. Everyone knows Axel's not interested in her. I've actually never seen Axel with a girlfriend. Not a playboy like you would expect though. He seems to keep to himself. Although, many would volunteer to fill that position in a heartbeat. Just look at him. Yummy." Hopping off the stool, she said, "I'll be right back. I'm going to the restroom."

Hating being alone for even a minute, I took a small sip of the drink I had been nursing and just watched. The group of men Axel hung with seemed so experienced and composed. They laughed and flirted, but still appeared powerful and dominating, even though it was obvious they were drinking and snorting white powder right off the table. They were cool, in a dark and fucked up way. And all I could do was almost knock the most desired person in the room down, and then fumble my way through a hopeless conversation. Even looking at them made me feel unworthy.

Sitting at the bar watching the "cool kids" made me miss home, particularly holing up in my office writing. Maybe I shouldn't have followed through with this crazy idea. Moving to LA and writing about something I knew absolutely nothing about. I wasn't prepared to feel so inadequate.

If Harrison hadn't talked me into this, I would be home with a glass of wine and a laptop as my only friend. Boring, maybe, but secure. I always listened to that man since he meant the world to me. He had become far more than just my editor. We'd been through so much over the years, last year especially when the nightmare of my sister's death almost destroyed me. Losing someone I had loved so dearly had left me leaning on my best friend Harrison as he stood by my side. I didn't really mind being alone with my words and my stories, but I appreciated having a friend who truly got me. Harrison understood my sheltered ways. He understood my past, and would stand by my side as we walked into the future… hopefully promoting a bestselling book. If I didn't fuck it all up, that is.

When I decided to move to LA to work on this book idea, Harrison and I made a promise to keep in touch daily. I wanted to make sure he helped me stay on task and gave me the encouragement to do something completely out of my comfort zone. So far, since I had made the move, we talked and texted every day, and I had a rough outline on my story already under way. No matter how caught up I got in this partying lifestyle, and then afterward immersing myself in writing the book, I was determined to keep Harrison in my life forever, both professionally and personally. This would be *our* project, and not just mine.

My goal was to get the info needed and write an incredible story, with Harrison to help edit and polish it into perfection. He then would shop it and find a home for it since I was far from having a literary agent to do it for me. Harrison had a much better grasp of what needed to happen and who to contact than I did.

I already had months' worth of research, mostly candid interviews with men and women who did drugs, frequented the clubs every chance they had, and with people who worked it like the bartenders and security. Between those and all the social media research, I was close to reaching my goal. I could then get back to the way I preferred my life. Safe, sound, and predictable. Just the way I liked it. LA, this club, and Axel Rye were just stepping stones to a brighter future. *If* I could land anything with Axel Rye, I was golden. Maybe I was shooting too big. I had only bumped into the man, but if I could dig up anything at all, then my book was all but sold.

My thoughts were interrupted when I felt the warmth from a sweaty body press up against me. I fought the urge to roll my eyes as I attempted to move away. A man with short-cropped hair, lacking a masculine bone in his pathetic frame, reached over to grab my hand.

"You seem like you're in a whole other world," he flirted.

"Just thinking. Getting ready to leave, actually."

He moved closer. "Do you want to go dance?"

I shook my head, not the least bit interested. "No, like I said, I'm getting ready to leave."

"Do you want to leave together?" he asked. "I'm ready to get out of here, too. I have some good shit I scored earlier we can take back to my place."

My eyes narrowed, and I leaned back as far away as I could from him. I had no desire to break it to him easy anymore. "I'm not interested. And I don't do drugs. Sorry."

The man leaned forward, and the stench of liquor on his breath overpowered my air space. "Well, then what are you doing in a place like this? Maybe you just need someone to show you what you're missing." He leaned in, and began putting his arms around my waist.

Feeling violated and disgusted all at the same time, I pushed him away. "I told you I'm not interested!"

Clearly annoyed, the man smirked and proceeded to move forward and force a hug. "Isn't that why you came tonight? To not be alone? To have some fun?"

"No. And even if I wanted to be with someone, it wouldn't be you!" I struggled to undo the asshole's hands that clasped behind my waist. And then, suddenly, the man was yanked off me. It took me a moment to understand what just happened before I realized someone had shoved him out of the way. To my surprise, my rescuer was Axel Rye.

What the fuck? Was this really happening?

"Get the hell away from her," Axel demanded, his eyes dark with fury.

The man's face went pale as he looked around to see who was watching. "Just a misunderstanding, dude." He quickly backed away and disappeared into the crowd without protest.

Axel turned to face me. I stood there wide-eyed and embarrassed by the commotion the incident had caused. "Are you okay?"

A few people noticed the scuffle and slowed as they walked by, but the disruption was not enough to call the attention of security. Thank God. The stares made me want to crawl off into a hole. I hated being the center of attention, especially negative attention. The entire night had just been one fuck up after another, and once again, I looked like an immature and stupid girl in front of the coolest man in the room.

I nodded. "Yes, thank you for being my knight in shining armor." I attempted to smile and wash away the fear. I was embarrassed to have so much attentiveness shown to me by Axel. I also hoped my boss wouldn't get wind of this. Off duty or not, I didn't think he'd be too happy about it. It would just be my luck to be fired in front of Axel to really add to my shame.

He chuckled. "I've never been called that before. More like a knight in fucked up armor." He took a minute to glance back at his buddies before staring at me. "But you are welcome."

An awkward silence sat between us. But everything about me felt pretty damn awkward.

"I feel bad for getting you involved. You didn't have to do that. He was just being a little too forward. I could've handled it." I craned my neck, looking for Felicity who had disappeared and missed the whole incident. I was trying my best to play it cool, even though I felt anything but.

"I'm sure you could've. I just don't like seeing men treat women like that. Women deserve respect. Sometimes in places like this, men can forget that simple fact."

I nodded, shrugged, and started toward the restrooms. I needed to get out of there fast before my failed attempt at small talk made me look like even more of an idiot. "I need to find my friend. I really do appreciate your help."

Axel followed beside me, walking close. My heart skipped when our hands touched for a mere moment. I tried to refocus my attention on finding Felicity and heading home. The night was long overdue to come to an end.

"Let me help you find her."

I noticed all the people in the VIP section now stared at us, especially Jillian. Axel seemed oblivious to the group. His eyes were fixed on me now. "No, it's all right. Really. I thank you for helping, but I don't want to keep you."

Axel reached out and softly placed his hand on my arm. The touch sent a shiver through my body. "If you are sure..." He paused and smiled. "I really hope to see you around."

I nodded, never looking Axel in the eye for longer than a moment. I worried I would say or do something stupid. "Thanks again for helping back there. I really appreciate it."

* * * * *

Axel

I couldn't help but stare at Quinn's eyes. No way was I letting her slip away. This could be my only shot, and I would kick myself if I let her walk away and then never saw her again. From her appearance and her overall vibe, she didn't seem like a club goer and this night was different for her and completely out of her norm. It was likely I would never see her again unless I did something about it. I don't know what it was, but something about this woman made me feel the need to be near her. I grabbed her hand as she turned away from me. It was soft and small, her fingers intertwining with my own. My heart pounded as she turned towards me. I tried focusing on something other than her eyes but found it impossible. She had the power to captivate with one simple look, sobering me with her stare.

"Would you like to go and hang out tomorrow night? I need to show up at another club called

Gaslight, and if you and your friend want to come, I would love to have you come along. It's an invite-only party, but I'll add you two to the list." I was sweating, nerves a foreign sensation for me. Maybe it was the coke, though deep down I knew my anxieties had nothing to do with what I snorted up my nose. "It's pretty hard-core, though. So I hope that doesn't bother you."

Quinn studied me for a moment, and then her voice cracked as she answered. "I can't. I'm working."

"Where do you work? Until what time?"

"I work here until eleven."

I smiled, loving what I heard. She must be a new hire. "You work here, huh? Well, I guess I'm going to see a lot more of you. I'm at this club a lot. What about after your shift? I don't usually show up at the other place until midnight, anyway."

"Okay, I'm sure Felicity would love it, too." Quinn broke her hand free from mine. "I really need to go, though. So, I'll see you tomorrow. *Gaslight* right?"

I nodded. "Yes, *Gaslight*. I will put you and…"

"Felicity Dexter."

"Okay, I will put your names on the list and see you there," I said, trying to keep my voice calm.

She nibbled her lip for a brief moment as if she were contemplating saying something, but then she nodded and left.

I stood staring after her as she walked away. Why did I feel like a love-struck schoolboy? Then it dawned on me. I hadn't actually asked a girl out in a very long time. I'd always just hooked up with someone at a bar or club since all of them sought *my* attention. I never had the desire to ask anyone out… until I met Quinn.

Chapter 3

Drink From The Fucked Up Bottle

Quinn

I sat in the kitchen, watching the phone, willing it to ring. I needed to talk to Harrison in the worst way. I'd already left a few texts and messages for him, and he still hadn't called me back. I tried to work on the initial outline of my story to keep my mind busy but couldn't focus long enough to even write a few words. Not to mention I found describing a club next to impossible. All my attempts kept sounding like some paranormal novel in an underground coven. I glanced at the clock as I typed the word "drug" again. Wishing I could come up with a different word, I realized I'd hit my writing wall for the day.

I jumped when the phone rang, grabbing it as fast as I could. "Hey, Harrison."

"It's good to hear your voice. How was your first day of work last night?"

"I've been dying to talk to you. You're never gonna guess what happened."

"What? You sound really happy."

I took a sip of my coffee before speaking. "I met Axel Rye last night. Not in the most glamorous of ways, but I met him."

"Axel Rye? The drug dealer?"

"I think we can say he is more than just a drug dealer, but yes. He wants me to hang out after work with him. He invited me to some exclusive club. I feel like I got the in already!" I continued to explain the details of the night, barely pausing to take a breath. I was more excited than I'd realized. "What if I actually get enough from him for my book? Can you imagine? An instant book deal right?"

"For sure." Harrison asked, "You gonna go tonight?"

"I'm not sure. I know I should for the book, but I'm scared shitless. To be honest, I feel so stupid around him and that entire crowd. They're completely above me. But I also know if I want to truly get the meat for my book... I guess I have to. But I'm not sure if I'm ready to dive in so quickly."

"Are you kidding me, Quinn? Shut up. This is your chance to have some fun out there and make some friends. This is also your chance to get the information you really need to make your story genuine. Not to mention Felicity will kill you if you say no. Stop living in your white, boring box. Axel Rye invited you, which is something most people would die for. So, you don't say no just because you are scared."

I smiled. Harrison was so good for me. He was forever my built-in cheerleader. He always had a way of making me feel good about myself and gave me the self-confidence I knew I lacked. "You don't understand. I've seen the women he hangs out with. They're so mysterious and sensual and... urban looking. Their style is their own. I honestly worry I'll look like a Plain Jane compared to them."

I stood up with the phone against my ear, then walked over and stood in front of the mirror. No tattoos, no piercings, nothing original about me. I looked at my less-than-exciting clothes and grimaced. Although I couldn't picture myself all tattooed and pierced, either.

"Who cares? Let me tell you something, Quinn. You need to stop thinking so little of yourself. I can guarantee you this group of women would die for your natural beauty. Axel asked you out for a reason. Stop knocking yourself down."

"I know. You're right." Hearing Harrison's advice caused me to miss him even more.

"You need to promise me something," he said.

I hesitated. "What?"

"You'll have a good time while you're out there. Don't limit yourself because you're scared or lack the confidence. Step out of your introverted self and live a little. And don't forget to take mental notes. You'll have your story sooner than you think."

"Okay, I'll try. But you're asking a lot. PJ bottoms, a glass of cheap chardonnay, and reality TV sounds pretty good right now."

"Quinn, I swear. Now, go get yourself ready, don't just put on black for the sake of it or so you can blend in, and have a good time. Let loose a bit."

* * * * *

Axel

We'd just left the restaurant, which was our first *request by owner* for the night, and we were all in good spirits as we rode in the limo to the club. Knox opened a bottle of Jack and began to pour everyone a drink, while Teddy started cutting lines on a mirror.

I tried not to groan. As much as I was trying to have a good time, I was tired and not really in the mood for partying. I'd never admit it to anyone, but the only reason I went at all tonight was for the possibility of seeing Quinn. She had been on my mind ever since last night. Hell, "consuming my thoughts" would be a better way to describe it.

The line outside the nightclub always made me feel odd. All these people patiently waited to get inside, when my crew and I would just waltz up to the door and be escorted in the minute we arrived. I knew it was all part of the scene and nightlife, but it made me feel arrogant. I swallowed the lump in the back of my throat, feeling my palms sweat against my whiskey glass. As we parked, everyone took turns snorting their lines and then began to move toward the limo door.

"Hold on, give me a sec," I said as I wiped at my nose after taking my line. I downed the whiskey as quickly as I could. I needed some artificial courage to kick in before I faced the night.

"Just bring the bottle with you," Teddy said, sniffing hard, and wiping away the residue of the coke beneath his nose. "I'm ready to get my party on."

I turned to Knox, who checked his image in the mirror one last time. His eyes were wide as saucers and blood shot, but I knew he didn't give a fuck less. Hell, I knew I looked the same, and just hoped Quinn didn't notice or, at the very least, care. I took another long swig of booze to help ease the flips going on inside my stomach. "All right, I'm ready." It wasn't the appearance that made me nervous, walking by all the club goers, or the fact that I had enough drugs on me to sell that could lock me up for the rest of my life, but rather who may be inside. The girl stole all my game.

Teddy reached for the door and put his classic meet-and-greet smile on. "Let's do this."

Knox and I laughed which sounded deep and distorted as the drugs kicked in and numbed my soul. I grabbed what was left of the Jack and followed him into the club.

* * * * *

Quinn

"They have viewing rooms here," Felicity informed me as she excitedly pulled me through the crowded club.

"Viewing rooms? What do you mean?"

"There are rooms where BDSM sex acts are going on. This will be great for your research! Talk about dark and gritty."

My heart skipped. "Wait. You want to go watch people have… sex? What's BDSM?"

Felicity continued to tug my resistant weight past dancing bodies. "Exactly! And you'll soon see." She reached into her pocket and pulled out a little plastic baggie. Inside were tiny little pink pills. "Here, take one of these. It will help you loosen up. You look like you are about to have a panic attack any minute."

I shook my head. "No, thanks. I don't do drugs."

"I know."

"What is it?"

"Just take it."

She put the pill to my mouth and pressed lightly. I could have turned my head, or resisted. I could have held my ground and refused to take the drug. But deep down, I didn't want to. I did want to loosen up. And I felt sick to my stomach at the thought of seeing Axel again, so maybe this would help. I didn't want to make a fool of myself again, and maybe this magic little pink pill could instantly turn me into one of the cool kids. It was worth a shot.

I opened my mouth and allowed Felicity to place the pill on my tongue. It tasted bitter, so I swallowed it as fast as I could. For a split second, I pictured how Alice in Wonderland drank from the bottle and could relate to the darkness of her tale. God that fairytale was really messed up. I only hoped I wouldn't be seeing a white rabbit running by me once the drug kicked in.

"Let's get a drink, and go watch some scenes get acted out. You're going to love it," Felicity said, tugging on my hand. "The bar is crowded. It's going to take forever to get something."

Maybe it took forever to get our drink. I don't know. Everything seemed like a blur, I was losing sense of time, and I still didn't see Axel.

Walking into the viewing room, I could smell the arousal. I could almost taste the sexual need of the raven-haired beauty splayed naked across the makeshift bed. Her ebony curls concealed parts of her breasts, allowing her hard nipples to peek between her cascading hair. Her pale body glistened in the colored club lights that swirled around her as she writhed in want.

Oh shit, the drugs were kicking in.

I felt lightheaded, hot, weak. The lights seemed to spread out in long lines. My ears felt as if they were clogged. My heart beat fast.

Shit. I was on drugs.

I was going to be like one of those characters in a *Lifetime* movie and die at a club.

Shit. I was going to die at a BDSM club and I didn't even know what that was!

Shit. Why did it feel like I was speaking my thoughts?

As if Felicity knew I was on the verge of calling 911 and telling them I was about to overdose, she whispered in my ear, "You're fine. It's just kicking in. Give it a minute, and it will even out. Just watch the scene and relax."

I nodded, and swallowed hard. A warmth oozed through me slowly, and I didn't exactly mind how I felt. I felt gooey but I liked it. I decided to do as Felicity instructed and I watched.

A gradual hush worked through the crowd as the bass music still pounded from the main room. I positioned myself near the exit so I could observe, but flee if it ended up being too intense. I watched in amazement as a man with a scarlet-red scarf around his neck walked into the room. He was obviously the person people wanted to see, the man who would act out the scene.

He closed his eyes as if taking in the energy, the smell, the passion rushing through the audience's veins. It was almost as if I knew this man could feel our desire, hear each breath we took, and taste the anticipation of the show to come. His dominance almost took my breath away.

Or was it the fucking drugs? Shit. I was high.

His dark brown hair rested slightly below his ears: his pale skin and ominous appearance gave him an aura that intrigued me. I watched the black jacket he wore sway as his body moved. The tight, black pants clung to his muscled thighs. His button-down white shirt revealed enough of his chest to make me and every audience member's mouth water in anticipation of glimpsing more. Watching his performance pulled at every sensation in my body. I wanted to run away, close my eyes, or do anything but stand in that room. On the other hand, my curiosity about the taboo won over.

"Master?" the woman on the bed questioned, her head lifting off the mattress to better view the man.

"No. I'm here to prepare you for his return," the man with the red scarf answered softly.

"I want Master."

"You will have him." The man moved to the bed. "Place your arms above your head," he commanded.

The dark-haired girl hesitated for a moment. Any doubt she may have had was overpowered by the seductive energy this man possessed. Her dark eyes twinkled with arousal as she gradually brought her hands over her head, laying her head down again. Her lips parted in desire, beckoning the man for the simplest of touches. She arched her back just enough to thrust out her hardened nipples, pleading for him to take them under his control. The man reached for each of her wrists, wrapped them with the red scarf from around his neck and tied them to the headboard of the bed. He then pulled two additional scarves from his pocket, grabbed each ankle and repeated the step of securing her to the bed.

"Kiss me," the woman begged as she gasped.

I could see the moisture along the soft folds of the woman's completely denuded pussy. She gyrated her hips in desperate need to be satisfied. I could only imagine how the woman felt. The sexual spell this room had on the spectators was all-powerful. It was an assumption, of course, but I could almost feel the craving, needing, longing, and desire that people felt as everyone watched. I could feel the pulsating between my own legs. Surprised by my feelings, I couldn't look away. I hungered for more.

The man slowly and seductively began to remove each item of his own clothing. Each movement of the man had the naked woman groaning for more. The girl's exposed pussy delicately dripped in anticipation for what he had in store.

"First rule is never command. You are *not* the one in charge." The man straddled the raven beauty and pressed his hard cock against her. "Your Master is the one to give commands. Only your Master."

I leaned over to Felicity who stared with open eyes. "Is this BDSM?"

"Shhh! Just watch."

The man lowered his mouth to the woman's hardened nipple and began to suck. He sucked and nibbled while softly massaging the girl's mound with the tip of his cock. He moved his mouth to the other nipple and continued to drive the girl to the edge of pleasure.

"More!" The girl begged as she flung her head in wild abandon.

The man reached down to the girl's pussy and briskly slapped the swollen folds. "I see you don't understand you are not the one in control. Your Master will not tolerate being told what to do." The man slapped the woman's pussy once again, releasing a moan from her. "You obviously need to be trained before his arrival."

"Yes, please," the dark-haired girl begged as she thrust her hips to meet the man's cock with more force.

What the hell was I watching? Was it the pill or was this shit real? Were people really doing this for all to see?

The man reached for a satin bag on the floor beside the bed. He pulled out what appeared to be some sort of small silver clamps yet seeing that they were adorned with small emeralds had me confused. Before I could lean towards Felicity again to ask about them, the man's intentions became clear.

I gasped and swallowed hard, shocked and yet somehow liking the idea of having what passed as erotic jewelry placed on the most intimate of places.

Still straddling the woman, the man grabbed one of her hardened nipples and very gently clasped the biting teeth. The woman let out a gasp as her back arched. I watched the slight grimace of pain on her face return to the sedated look of pleasure. The man bent down and softly placed his lips to the nude beauty's mouth, giving a kiss as a reward for her ability to accept the jewelry.

"Very good," the man whispered between the kiss.

He slowly lowered his lips to the other nipple and lightly licked along the surface. Grabbing the other clamp, the man tenderly applied it to her nipple, allowing it to join the other.

I almost gasped as I took in the magnificent sight of the sexual woman writhing only a few feet away. The silver, the jewels, her breasts, and the beginning of her submission were breathtaking. I loved watching how the man had the power to dominate, the power to control, and the power to please. I was learning how one could demand another's ecstasy.

I briefly closed my eyes and slowly took in the aroma of the girl's sex as the man lowered his mouth to the woman's wanting pussy. Pressing his tongue lightly to skin bared but for the droplets of her arousal, he began to lick his way up and down the folds of the dripping-wet mound. He danced his tongue in a circle around her clit, causing the girl's moans to become more of a scream. The man pressed his finger past the entrance of her pussy, pulling out to reveal the wet heat of the girl's passion.

"That feels so good... so good," the woman moaned.

The man hooked his finger into the depths of the girl's pussy and reached for the satin bag once again. He pulled out an item I instantly could name though it was nothing like I'd ever seen before. This was a clear glass dildo that had two leather straps lined with crystals attached. The man took the clear penis and rubbed it along the girl's wet pussy, collecting her moisture. Ever so gently, he replaced his finger with the large dildo. Once he had the dildo snugly in her depths, he placed the straps around the girl's thighs, securing the toy in place.

The woman gasped at the intrusion and began to gyrate her hips in desperation. "Fuck me. Make me come. I need to come!"

Without pause, the man flipped the girl onto her stomach. "I warned you about issuing the commands." He swatted the girl's creamy white behind. "You are to submit, you are to accept, you are to surrender." He spanked the girl's ass again. "You are to do only as your Master, and those he deems fit, requests... nothing more."

He grabbed yet another item from the satin bag. Pulling out another phallus, yet this one had my brow furrowing. It was smaller than the dildo he'd seated inside her. And it wasn't glass but appeared to be steel. I watched as he rubbed the emerald that decorated the base with the tip of his finger. Smaller diamonds circled the emerald, making it sparkle in the swirling lights of the club. I loved the intricate workmanship of this toy above all. Using the woman's wetness from her pussy, I gasped again as the man lubricated the girl's tight hole with his finger. In and out, slowly, he stretched the girl's anus, so she would be able to accept the last of the jewelry. I assumed the Master would be pleased with the jeweled items chosen, as well as the frenzied state his submissive was in.

"I want you to relax," he ordered as he placed a soft kiss on the reddened ass of the woman.

I watched in awe as the man pressed the steel plug past the tight ring of her ass. The woman moaned and bucked against the mattress as he continued to press it inside until only the jeweled base remained visible. The man rolled her over onto her back and took a moment to admire the jeweled beauty before him.

He bent down and pressed his lips to the woman's mouth one last time. "Very nice. You did very well. Your Master will be pleased."

Holy shit! I was fucking high.

* * * * *

Axel

We walked to the front door, past the bouncer and the red rope. There were a lot more people than we'd expected. A fairly big-name DJ played at the venue tonight, so the promo was pretty large. We started making our way through the crowd. I had just begun to scan the place when I saw her. She stood by the doorway of one of the viewing rooms. She looked embarrassed and out of her element. I could see interest, and even a hint of arousal, but I also saw something different. I couldn't put my finger on it. Quinn seemed out of place.

I swallowed hard. Quinn's long hair flowed more than halfway down her back. Her jeans hugged her body, and she wore a pair of worn leather boots. Her magenta-colored blouse clasped around her neck, backless except for the bottom part that clung securely around the small of her tantalizing back. Quinn Sullivan… was anyone more captivating?

I put the rim of the Jack bottle to my mouth, taking another small swig. Originally I had wanted to be careful not to drink too much, and wanted to stay clear of the blow for at least tonight. My friends, Teddy and Knox, would make up for me when it came to the cocktail and drug consumption. They always did. I wanted to make a good impression on Quinn. I found it hard enough to keep my senses intact around her as it was. But I fucked that up, and now I was already down the rabbit hole.

I leaned into Knox's ear to shout above the loud, booming music. "I'll be back. There's someone I need to go see."

Knox acknowledged me with a nod. "I'm going to go get a drink. You want one?"

"I'm good, thanks." I held up my bottle of Jack, still half full.

Walking in Quinn's direction, I recognized the short raven-haired girl holding a cocktail with Quinn as her friend from last night, Felicity.

As I approached Quinn, I could feel my heart pick up tempo and my gut clench. Despite my efforts to quiet my nerves artificially, I felt completely on edge. It surprised the hell out of me. I prided myself on my confidence with the ladies. Control at all times dictated my demeanor. One look at this woman changed all of that.

I walked around behind her and moved in closer. She smelled wonderful, giving off a gentle floral fragrance. Not suffocating or unbearable like some of the women's perfume I was used to smelling. No stench of alcohol, no stale cigarette smoke, no sweaty-club-atmosphere-odor present. Everything about Quinn refreshed my senses. My old self had become stale, and she gave me a renewed awareness.

I hungered to wrap my arms around her tiny frame and hold onto her like she belonged to me. Instead, against my will, I eased closer and talked in her ear. "Hey, I'm glad you decided to come."

Quinn spun around, nearly spilling her drink all over me. Her expression went immediately from startled, to embarrassed, to welcoming. Her smile beckoned like a lighthouse. "Yeah, I'm glad, too. What a great place. I had no idea it would be so crowded." Her smile continued to draw me in. "Felicity was really excited when I told her we were invited. Thank you."

I couldn't get over how stunning she looked. If I stared at her every day of my life, it would never be enough. The word "captivating" was created for this woman. "I had no idea your hair was so long. Last night you had it pulled up and… you have beautiful hair."

Quinn paused for a second. "Thank you." I noticed she avoided eye contact again, reminding me of last night. Her eyelashes actually appeared to rest against her cheekbones, the blush rising underneath.

I cast my eyes over her shoulder at the sex scene going on behind her and asked, "Are you liking what you see?"

She instantly looked into my eyes and then back down at the ground, clearly embarrassed by the question. I had seen just enough of her eyes to see she was high, which for some odd reason was like a sucker punch to the gut. I didn't want my perfect, innocent, Quinn Sullivan doing drugs like all the others. She had been sober last night, but tonight she wasn't. "I uh, Felicity uh... I don't normally..." But now I could see. This wasn't normal for her. It was obvious.

It was easy to see the conversation made Quinn uncomfortable, and I was afraid she would want to run off. I had no intentions of letting her run away again. Not this time. I glanced at her glass. "What are you drinking?"

She smiled timidly. "I have no idea."

"What? You don't know what you're drinking?"

She laughed. "No clue. Felicity handed it to me. It's good, though."

Quinn's smile somehow had a calming effect on me. "Well, would you like another drink of 'I have no idea', or would you like to try 'beats me?' "

She laughed even louder. "Ooh, I love 'beats me!' That drink's amazing."

I found her sense of humor refreshing, especially since she seemed so shy. The contrast only added to the hold this woman had on me. Whatever the magic was, I was spellbound.

"Um, Axel," she said, once again looking at the ground. "I'm sorry. I'm a little out of it right now. This is so not like me."

I nodded and put my hand softly on her arm. "It's okay. I think everyone in this room is a little out of it." I leaned in. "Are you feeling okay?"

She looked up and gave another one of her captivating smiles. "I feel really good. Almost too good."

I chuckled. "Well good. Let me go get you that drink. I'll be right back."

I quickly ordered the drink, never taking my eyes off of her. I was happy that the bartender served me instantly so I could return to her as quickly as possible. "Here you go."

Quinn reached for Felicity's hand as the scene in the room had come to an end. "I haven't introduced you yet. This is my friend, Felicity. I just moved out here a few days ago from San Francisco, and she's been kind enough to let me stay with her."

I nodded. "Yes, I've seen Felicity around."

Felicity's eyes widened slightly in surprise. "You have?"

I nodded again. "Let's just say you may have a secret admirer."

"What? Who?" Felicity reminded me of a little girl at Christmas.

"Sorry. My lips are sealed." I wasn't about to tell her that Knox had been eyeing her for quite some time. He thought she was hot as fuck but hadn't made his move yet.

Quinn gave a playful wink as she took a small sip of her drink. Felicity looked as if she were about to speak when another girl who had just made her way to where they stood, pulled her away.

I decided I had had enough of the Jack and placed the bottle on a table nearby. I watched Quinn intently. Her body was so small, but she looked so strong. Her perfect pout begged to be kissed... almost demanded. The demand was more powerful than any command a Dom in this club could issue. My loins constricted as I pictured me kissing her. Obsession at its highest.

"So, did you come here alone?" Quinn asked.

I looked toward my friends in the center of the room. I had to. If I stared at her any longer, I feared I'd cause her to seek the next exit. I felt like a crazed stalker or something.

"No, my friends are here somewhere, working the room, earning their money." I turned back to Quinn. "Someone needs to earn our paycheck."

She sipped on her drink again. "What exactly is it you do?" Quinn held my gaze for a moment and then smiled, making my heart skip.

"Do you really not know?" I asked.

She blushed and looked down at the ground. "I guess I do." She looked up into my eyes. "Do you like dealing drugs?" She cleared her throat and shifted her weight from one foot to the other. "I'm sorry. That was a stupid and nosey question. Like I said, my brain isn't really working right now."

"It's okay. And to answer your question—not really."

"You don't like it?"

I shrugged. "It pays the bills. It just really isn't who I am."

She smiled again. "Who are you?"

I stood there, enthralled with every word and every move Quinn made, wondering how I could answer her question, when I felt a tap on my shoulder. It was Knox. "Hey, we're going to take off."

I looked at Quinn. She seemed so small and delicate and incredibly vulnerable. Or I was just going to use that as my excuse for wanting to stay with her. "I'm going to stick around. Her friend left, and I don't want to leave her alone."

Quinn smiled at me. "Go ahead, I'm fine."

"I'm not going to leave you here by yourself. I'll stay with you until Felicity gets back."

Quinn grabbed my hand, and pulled me into the crowd of dancing bodies. "Come on, let's go look for Felicity so you feel comfortable going with your friends." She smiled softly at me, making my heart melt even more—if that was even possible.

As we made our way across the dance floor, one of Jillian's friends tried to stop me. "Hey, Axel, where's Jillian? She was supposed to be here tonight. Didn't she come here with you?" Her eyebrows arched, and she peered at Quinn. I kept walking, pretending not to hear.

"Is Jillian your girlfriend?" I could feel Quinn try to let go of my hand but I only tightened the grip.

I shook my head. "No, not at all."

We continued to make our way through the club, no sign of Felicity appearing. Knox caught up with us, looking a little irritated.

"Axel, come on. Let's get out of here," Knox insisted.

Quinn still held my hand. I looked at her apologetically, and then turned to Knox. "Give me a sec. She needs to find her friend before I'm comfortable leaving."

Quinn smiled, finally looking deep into my eyes. "I'll be fine. Go ahead. Don't make your friends wait because of me."

It took all my willpower to not lean over and kiss her, but the last thing I wanted was for anything to happen tonight that would scare Quinn away. She seemed timid, and as much as I found it sexy as hell, I didn't want to come off as too aggressive.

"Oh, hey," I said, addressing Knox. "This is Quinn. Quinn, this is my friend, Knox."

Quinn blushed slightly and said hello in a tentative voice. I knew Knox assumed she was just some girl I'd picked up at the club for a quick hookup.

We all made our way to the exit, where Teddy stood with arms crossed, waiting. Quinn couldn't find Felicity at all. She had tried to send her some texts, as well as calling her several times, with no response.

Quinn frowned at her phone. "Something wrong?" I asked.

"Can we leave? Do you mind taking me home?"

"What about Felicity?" I asked.

"I'll send her a text letting her know I got a ride home. Felicity sometimes hooks up with a guy and forgets about who she came with." Quinn shrugged.

"I just don't want to be here by myself. Can I get a ride with you?"

I stared at her for a second, delighted to have more time with her. "That sounds like a good idea. You definitely shouldn't be here alone... feeling a little off." I gave her a playful wink.

I finally let go of Quinn's hand. I placed my palm on her lower back and escorted her out of the club to our awaiting limo. I helped her into the seat and sat down next to her, reaching for her hand immediately. Both Knox and Teddy studied my actions, no doubt shocked to see me give anyone affection, something I never did. They did... but not me. It was a definite change of pace having them leave the club empty handed, but with me having someone by my side.

"Have the driver drop us off first," Knox said, motioning toward Teddy. "Then you can take Quinn home."

I smiled, relieved Knox made it easy for me to have some alone time with Quinn. I wasn't ready to say goodnight to her yet. I could always count on Knox to help a guy out.

Chapter 4

Fucked Up Resume

Quinn

Listening to the ringtone while I sat in the limo, heart pounding, I waited for Felicity to answer. The fresh air, and leaving the loud music of the club helped sober me up. I felt relaxed, and really good. But I no longer felt I was so high that I needed to crawl in a ball up against a wall. The edge was gone, and for that I was grateful.

"Hello?"

"Felicity?"

"Quinn, I've been looking for you. Where are you? Are you okay?"

"I'm with Axel. I couldn't find you, so I decided to get a ride home with him. Are you on your way home?"

"No, I met a friend and we're going to go to another club. Do you need me to come get you? Do you want to come?" Felicity asked.

"No, I'll have Axel take me home."

"I can't believe you are with Axel Rye! You're living the dream, girl."

Her words made my heart beat even harder. I bit my lip.

I decided to ignore the comment. "I'll see you when you get home. Be safe."

"Is he right there next to you?" Felicity whispered, as if Axel might hear her.

I giggled. "You have fun tonight."

"You *have* to hook up with him! And I want to hear all about it."

I laughed nervously, my face suddenly warm. "Felicity!" I whispered. "I'll be fine. Bye."

"Let loose! Give it a shot; you might surprise yourself." Yeah, the last time I listened to her and let loose, my body felt it was going to melt while I watched a man perform acts I never knew possible.

My pulse sped up. Felicity didn't help my already strained nerves. "I gotta go. Have a good night." I hung up the phone, trying not to notice Axel watching me.

After dropping everyone off, Axel turned to me and smiled. That smile. It was unlike anything I had seen. It was soft, sensual, and alluring. I shifted in my seat, trying not to appear anxious, but I found it nearly impossible to control my nervous energy. Why was I having such a hard time breathing now?

"Are you hungry?" Axel asked.

I let out the breath I was holding and nodded.

"Good, because I'm starving." He leaned forward to the driver and muttered some instructions.

We picked up some food at a small coffee shop and headed to the beach, eating along the way in the back seat. I hadn't realized how hungry I truly was until I bit into my sandwich. Everything about the meal and the company was perfect. Axel had a way of making me feel warm, comforted, and relaxed. I ate more than I would normally and talked more about myself than I would ever do. I guarded my past, my present, and my future. I opened up to very few, and had found it was easier that way. It wasn't like I had anything exciting to really open up about. My insecurities always had me thinking before that people were judging me for being so boring. I did, however, open up slightly to Axel. I felt comfortable enough to discuss my likes and dislikes. I had told him my favorite color, my favorite food, what music I liked, what movie last made me cry. It must have been that little pink pill, but I was talking a mile a minute.

I took the last bite of my sandwich and leaned back against the leather of the limo seat. "I'm so full, I could explode!"

Axel smiled warmly. "From the looks of it, you could add a few pounds to that frame of yours."

I blushed. "Yeah, I tend to skip meals. I get caught up in work and forget, I guess. I lose track of time." When I'd write, hours would fly by.

Axel raised an eyebrow. "Bartending?"

Crap! I had almost given away that I was a writer.

I just shrugged casually. "I needed the sandwich. I feel so much better. My brain seems to be coming back."

"What exactly did you take?"

I knew I was blushing. I shouldn't feel weird for doing drugs. Axel was a drug dealer for Christ's sake, but I totally felt like he would judge me. "I don't know. It was pink."

"A pink pill?"

"Yes."

"You just took a pink pill and didn't know what it was?" His eyes darkened, and he didn't look as jovial as he had been before.

"Felicity gave it to me." I shrugged. "I trust her."

He nodded slowly and his expression seemed to soften. "Well you need to be careful with that shit. I didn't sell it to her, so who knows where she got it. It could be dirty."

I laughed. "As opposed to clean drugs? Are there such things? If she would have bought the pink pill from you, would it then be good for me?"

He stopped for a moment and then let out a deep and hearty laugh. "Good point. Fine. Drugs are bad, little girl. Stay away!"

We laughed until a silent calm washed over us as we both just looked at each other. Axel's eyes were soft and gentle. He casually had one arm slung over the back of the seat, giving off a sense of comfort and a perception of ease. I realized we were both staring at each other, and I began to grow uneasy.

"So where are we going?" I asked to change up the mood.

Axel took a moment to continue to stare. "To one of my favorite places in the city. Believe it or not, the clubs are my least favorite part."

"What do you mean?"

"They aren't me."

I almost laughed. "You do realize you are Axel Rye, right? Your name alone represents these clubs."

Axel frowned. "I know, and I hate that."

I smiled softly and straightened my back. "Then why do you do it?"

Axel's face grew serious. "That's a good question. I guess I'm searching."

I took a deep breath to attempt to soothe my nerves. "Searching?"

Axel reached across the seat and lightly grabbed my hand. He didn't say anything, but his soft touch made me feel calm and relaxed again. He gave a gentle squeeze before pulling his hand away.

Axel and I sat in silence again. I noticed how easy it was for both of us to sit and be content in each other's company. We both could stare into each other's eyes, taking the time to observe. I liked how Axel's eyes would light up when he smiled. I liked how he was confident enough not to look away. I liked how he had a way of holding my stare, demanding my eyes stay connected with his. I liked… well, I liked Axel.

"So, tell me something about you. I feel you have the upper hand because you know so much about me. I feel like I haven't stopped talking this whole drive." This was my chance to start building my story.

"I have no secrets. What would you like to ask?"

"I can ask anything?"

Axel smiled. "Yes, you can ask anything."

I took a moment to think of a good question. I wasn't sure if I would get this opportunity to ask anything of my liking again. I also wanted to be careful not to come across as a reporter or something.

"Okay, so why is a good-looking man, like you, not in a serious relationship?" I blushed at how forward I sounded but continued. "You have to give me honesty, nothing simple or general."

Axel smirked. "So saying I haven't met the right woman is considered general?"

"Yes."

Axel took a moment to just stare into my eyes. His eyes narrowed a bit and his jaw tightened. "I'm darker than most."

I shook my head. "No, that was way too simple of an answer. And cliché. Of course the famous Axel Rye who sells drugs for a living is darker than most."

"I live in a world not cut out for the average person."

I shook my head again. "Nope, that was too general."

"I'm fucked up."

I pouted out my lip. "You can't just give broad, elusive answers. Not fair!"

Axel chuckled. "Okay, okay. You are pretty damn cute when you pout." He took a deep breath and repositioned his body against the back seat. "Well, I think it is no secret I sell drugs. Actually, it's more than that. I am *known* for selling drugs. I used to just be the rich kid of Jamison Rye, but I made a name for myself." He paused and studied me intently for a moment before huffing with a smirk. "Some name."

"Why?" I asked in a soft voice. I wanted to know for more than just my book. "What made you decide to start selling drugs?"

Axel thought for a moment. "I'm not sure how it happened really. I was a cocky kid with unlimited money, and power. For a teenager, being allowed in any club just because my last name was Rye was pretty cool. I hung with rock stars, actors, models, you name it. It started with me just providing my friends with drugs, and then I had the hook up." He paused as if thinking. "It just sort of happened. Before I knew it, I was making major money and was in demand at every single club in LA."

"And then you got arrested?" I asked, careful not to have any judgment in my voice.

"Yeah. I'm assuming you are talking about the latest stint. I got arrested many times before. But it was always a slap on the wrist or Daddy used his money and lawyers to get me off. But this last one was pretty scary. They were talking about serious jail time. Lucky for me, I had an excellent team of lawyers."

"Why do you still do it? Aren't you scared of getting caught and going to jail again?" I asked.

Axel shook his head. "No. The District Attorney ended up looking like a fool. And let's just say that my lawyers, private investigators and fixers were able to dig up enough dirt on people to forever keep me out of jail." He chuckled. "The sex scandals, the drugs, the dark side of people who are supposed to be the good guys is pretty fucked up. It's like fucking mafia shit I'm talking about. And I can't tell you how many people have bought from me. Needless to say, I'm off limits unless some powerful people want to go down with me." He shrugged and looked disappointed. "I'm not proud that Daddy's money bailed me out. Hell, I'm not proud that my fucking legacy is a bad boy drug dealer either. But it is what it is."

I looked at Axel skeptically. "You say that like you are trapped. Like you don't have a choice in the matter."

"What else am I going to do with my life? I dropped out of high school, and actually have no skills. I know one thing and that is the nightlife. I am a professional partier. How's that for a fucked up resume?"

"Are you happy?"

He shook his head. "No, I'm over this shit. But like I said, what else is there? This is literally all I know. But I do like my friends, and it could be a hell of a lot worse. I could be working some blue-collar job I hate just as much, and be struggling every month just to pay the bills. I have a pretty good gig. I get paid a lot of money to party, pass out party favors, and make a trendy spot to appear even hotter. Many people would be grateful to be in my shoes, and I have to remind myself of that. This is who I am. I own it."

I just sat and stared at Axel while he spoke. He had such passion and conviction in his voice. He seemed so centered and focused. Everything about Axel screamed strength and stability. I had never heard someone be so open in admitting they sell drugs for a living. I had read articles about his court appearance and his history, but the information seemed so shallow compared to actually hearing it from Axel. I wasn't appalled or shocked. I didn't think he was a bad man, or criminal. I respected him for his ability to be honest and straightforward. Now, I had to figure out how to make my readers feel the same way. I had to capture this side of Axel Rye for the book, or I would be doing everyone a disservice.

Axel stopped and stared at me. He furrowed his eyebrows and sat up straight against the seat. "What are you thinking?"

I smiled and cleared my throat. "I think you live an interesting life. I like that you aren't ashamed of it, and you wear who you are on full display. I admire that." Did I? Or was I saying it for the sake of my undercover mission? This all would make a great book.

Axel looked shocked. He leaned forward and asked, "You do? You don't think I should be locked up for breaking the law every single night?"

"Nope, it's who you are. You aren't forcing anyone to buy and take the drugs." I blushed and shyly said, "Honestly, I've never taken drugs in my life until tonight."

Axel paused and looked slightly uncomfortable for the first time since I had met him. He fidgeted in his seat for a few moments before taking a deep breath to control his demeanor again. I watched in curiosity at his reaction.

"I know this is going to sound hypocritical, but I really hope you stay away from the drugs," Axel confessed. "It's dangerous. I have seen so many people become addicted and ruin their lives. I guess you could say that *I* ruined their lives."

"Well you don't have to worry about me. I'm just having a little fun and relaxing a bit. I've always been so straight laced. I like letting loose around you. Maybe you are making me into a bad girl." I giggled and blushed the minute the words left my mouth. I was flirting, and I couldn't help it.

Axel smiled so big that wrinkles formed around the corners of his eyes and a slight dimple took shape in his cheek. "So you are a bad, bad girl heh?"

"Yes, yes, I think I am." I continued to flirt. "But you are a bad, bad, boy."

For a moment, Axel and I stared deep into each other's eyes again. I searched for some further explanation. I searched for some clarity as to why I felt so incredibly turned on by what he just confessed to. He was a bad boy drug dealer and I liked it. He sat on the wrong side of the law like an outlaw in some old western. It pulled me in.

He sat on the other side of the limo refusing to break the stare. Feeling uncomfortable and a bit insecure at his intensity, I broke the stare first. I looked down at my hands and felt his glare burn my already red-hot skin.

Taking a moment before looking back into Axel's eyes, I asked, "So you have more money than you know what to do with, girls hanging on your every move, and are the son of rock star. Oh, and you just happen to sell drugs to every cool kid in town."

He laughed. "You just described me to a T. Quite the catch right? Women are just lining up to settle down and be in a long term relationship with me. Nothing says stability and retirement like marrying a drug dealer. I haven't found someone who wants the same things: drugs, booze, flocks of groupies, media attention, legal issues, and vampire hours."

"I find it hard to believe that with the crowd you hang out with you haven't met a woman who wants the same, or at least gets you."

Axel frowned. "Groupies. That's all they are. They either want the fame, the free access to everywhere cool in town, or the free drugs. In most cases they want all of it." Axel paused and looked directly into my eyes. "That's definitely not what I want." He let out a big sigh. "So did I do my part on the sharing game? Did I answer all your questions?"

I nodded as his stare sent a chill down my spine. "Yes, you did. Thank you."

"Thank you for asking. No one has cared enough to ask."

After driving up a winding street to the top of a hill, the limo turned into a dead end and parked. The moon was bright, and the ocean went on as far as I could see. The view of the boats floating in the distance stole my breath.

I stared out the window in amazement. This was the first time I'd gotten to really take in the city I now lived in.

Axel reached for my hand and opened the door. "Follow me." He got out of the limo, gently assisting me to do the same.

I kept my hand in Axel's as we walked to a stone wall. I could see the waves crashing onto the rocks below. We walked a little further to a space with benches and a grassy sitting area with flowers planted in brick flower beds. I took it all in with awe. I turned back to Axel.

"It's beautiful," I whispered.

"This is my favorite place."

"I can see why. It's nice to see this side of LA. All I've seen really are the bar and clubs." I stepped closer to the wall and gazed out into the black ocean. The lights on a couple of ships and some small boats shined brightly against the blackness of the water. It had rained earlier, so the ground was still wet, but the sky had mostly cleared. Axel walked up behind me and placed his hands on top of the water-soaked stone, enclosing my body between his arms. His body heat against my back warmed my skin, contrasting to the nippy weather outside. Axel rested his chin on my shoulder next to my ear, taking a deep breath. Every move he made exuded confidence. He never hesitated or seemed unsure. I closed my eyes as my body tingled all over. Taking my own deep breath, I tried to quiet my escalating nerves. I found it unbelievable that I was here, doing this, with Axel... a man I felt as if I already knew.

"I love the way you smell," Axel murmured, his breath hot against my neck.

"Thank you." They were the only words I could squeak out.

We stood there for a few minutes in silence, his breath searing against my soul. Finally, he spoke. "Can I ask you something?"

The question and the intensity of the situation made me nervous. "Yes."

Axel tightened his arms around my body more.

"Why do you seem so anxious around me? Do I make you uncomfortable?"

I went stiff. I thought I had been doing so well keeping my emotions hidden. "I'm just not the best in new situations. I can be shy, I guess." Even my explanation seemed anxious. I was making it worse.

Axel placed his hands over my shaking ones on the wall. "There's something about you that I really like, Quinn. Am I crazy, or do you feel the connection, too?"

I squeezed my eyes shut for a second. Shit, I'm in this for the story. I didn't want to tell Axel that. I didn't want Axel to know. He would assume I was using him for a paycheck. And the reality was, that I was! His story was gold and my sure ticket to getting a publishing deal. I knew this. I had to stay focused, but my heart and body were at war with my mind.

"I'm not sure what I'm feeling." I felt confused. I had never been interested in a man like him. I liked normal. I liked safe. I liked everything opposite of Axel Rye. But for some reason I stood there in Axel's arms, not stopping it.

"I want to see where this takes us."

Alta Hensley

I braced myself, not knowing how he would feel about me after I confessed why I was really in LA, and why I was really trying to get close to him. Was I leading him on? Had I made Axel believe I was interested? The bigger question being... was I interested in Axel?

I turned around, but he never let go of the wall, keeping me encircled in his hold. His eyes seemed darker somehow, sultry. He looked straight at me, waiting.

"What do you mean?" My heart pounded. Overwhelming confusion clouded my brain.

"Are you seeing anyone?" His eyes remained fixed on mine.

I shook my head. "No."

"Good." Axel smiled. "Then you're free."

My eyebrows shot up. "Free for what?" I could feel something; an intensity I'd never felt before from anyone. He stood so close to me, I could feel every breath he took.

"To explore this connection." He dropped his hands from the stone, and placed them around my waist. With my heart pounding against my chest, I swallowed hard, wondering if Axel could see how he affected me.

"Can I kiss you?" he asked in a soft whisper.

I nodded, unable to say a word. Axel didn't hesitate and gently placed his lips against mine. They were soft and warm, softer than any kiss I had ever had. Axel explored my mouth slowly, with the most delicate touch. He tightened his grasp around my waist with one arm, and brought his other hand up to caress my cheek. With a velvet stroke, Axel's hand wrapped around my neck, pulling the kiss even deeper.

With Axel's body pressed strong against mine, I was surprised to feel his broad chest up against my own. His tongue moved faster, with more passion, and with more need. I had never kissed liked this before. This kiss was new, exciting, tantalizing, and burned to my inner core. Never had I kissed with so much passion and sensuality. Never had I longed to explore beyond the kiss so much. Never had I imagined a kiss could pull out such strong emotions.

It was too much. The passion grew, the breathing turned to pants, gasps turned to moans, and I panicked. I pulled away, burying my face into Axel's hair.

Caressing my back, Axel took a moment to soothe me before backing away slowly. He looked deep into my eyes. "Let's go sit down."

We walked over to a wooden bench underneath a huge tree. We both sat, turning so we faced each other.

Axel stared at me and smiled, highlighting the sexy scar near his lip. "You really are pretty, you know that?" He leaned forward and placed a very soft peck on my lips. "So, you said you're from San Francisco. Why did you decide to move here?"

I straightened up a little, suddenly feeling on edge. Talking about reality was popping the wonderful fairy-tale bubble I had been in. I didn't want the moment to end. "I haven't exactly moved here. It's just temporary."

"Why is it only temporary?"

I shrugged. "Just staying for a while to figure out my future… I guess." I glanced at Axel, hoping we could move on to another subject. I wanted the bubble back.

"How long do you plan on staying?"

I looked out into the night sea and just shrugged again. "I'm not sure. Just playing it by ear."

Axel was silent for a moment. He examined me, eyes full of questions.

"Is there anyone back home to return to?" he asked.

"My sister died not that long ago, and that left me with a pretty broken family. My sister and I were raised by our parents who were only children, so I've always had a really small family. Now, other than my parents who are sort of dealing with their dark crap, I just have some acquaintances and my really close friend Harrison. He's the closest thing I have to a normal family right now. He's been in my life for a long time. But we've never been anything more than friends, as crazy as that might sound. People find it hard to believe men and women can just be friends. It also helps that he's gay."

I noticed how intently Axel watched me when I spoke, as if he didn't want to miss a single word.

"I don't think it sounds crazy at all. I have women friends. Friendship doesn't always have to involve sexuality." Axel looked at me thoughtfully and put his arm around my waist. "Well, until you leave, I'd still like to explore this connection we have. That kiss only confirmed my feelings that you and I may have something."

I stared at him, speechless.

Axel smiled. "Let's not think of the future and you leaving anymore. Let's focus on right now."

His lips were on mine again. I allowed myself to close my eyes and just take in the moment. I allowed the feelings of passion, desire, and need to rock my body. I didn't fight the emotions with any doubt or confusion. I allowed the kiss to be just that. An amazing, affectionate, and life-altering kiss.

Chapter 5

Freaked The Fuck Out

Quinn

I couldn't remember the last time I'd felt so alive. Soaking in the bath with the warm water blanketing my body, I thought of Axel as I lathered my skin. The feelings rushing through me scared me as much as they thrilled me. This was Axel, the famous Axel Rye that I'd heard so much about. This was a man known for selling drugs. This was a man who hadn't left my thoughts since last night.

My body quivered at the memory of the kiss. So gentle, yet so passion-filled. Axel's lips and tongue were softer than any kiss before. His touch was more tender and sensitive. The kiss tantalized and seduced my very core. Never had I imagined kissing someone would stir up so much intensity. Confusion mixed with desire as I sat and fantasized of what was yet to come.

The first thing I did last night when I got home was call Harrison. I had told him everything, not wanting to leave anything out, especially about the kissing. Harrison hadn't been surprised at all that Axel was interested in me. He was happy I sounded so excited, but warned me to take it slow, although it already seemed we were in overdrive and I really had no control of the speed. Harrison had told me not to overthink everything and not make it more dramatic then it needed to be. Kissing did not make an instant future. Harrison always had a way of calming me down.

I climbed out of the bath and dressed. After getting ready, I walked into the kitchen to find Felicity sitting at the table, eating her morning cereal and drinking coffee.

"Where are you going so early?" she asked, looking shocked to find me already ready to go.

My cheeks warmed. "Axel's coming to get me." I tried not to blush any more.

Felicity's eyes widened and her jaw dropped. "Oh really?"

I nodded, unable to hide the smile. I walked over to the coffee pot and poured myself a cup of coffee with Felicity staring in disbelief. "I can't believe you're going out with Axel Rye again. Details, details!" She said his name almost in a sing-song-like tone.

I sat down at the table across from her. I didn't want to make a big deal out of it. The more I made out of this now, the harder it would be if this all turned out to be nothing or if I was just another girl to Axel. A small amount of pain attacked my heart just thinking about it. But I knew it was a definite possibility.

"Nothing much to say," I said. "I'm trying not to overthink the whole thing. It is what it is."

Felicity rolled her eyes. "Please. Don't give me that line of crap. I know you well enough to know when you're withholding the full truth," she said.

"We hung out one night. There's nothing to this."

"I'm telling you, there is. You're in uncharted territory. Does he know you're working on the book?"

"No. I don't see why that matters. We just hung out." I could feel myself getting defensive.

"I think you haven't said anything because you're interested in Axel, and you're pretty sure he wouldn't go for it." She smiled. "I don't blame you."

I shrugged and took a sip of coffee. "Well, like I said, this is no big deal—"

"Yet," Felicity interrupted. "We'll see how quickly you guys get serious."

"What makes you so sure we'll be getting serious? You yourself said he's never had a girlfriend. And have you forgotten about his lifestyle? I can't exactly get serious with a fucking drug dealer now can I?"

It was almost a rhetorical question. I didn't really want to hear the answer. Felicity made this too stressful. It was way too soon to start worrying about what Axel really wanted out of all of this.

Felicity leaned back in the kitchen chair and crossed her legs. "We'll see. Mark my words, you guys will be a full-blown couple soon. You'll be fucking by the end of the week."

I almost choked on my coffee. "Felicity! Jesus!"

"I'm just saying." She laughed.

* * * * *

Axel

I pulled up to the house and was getting out of the car when I saw Quinn come out the door. Immediately, I smiled like a silly schoolboy. She was having that continued effect on me. I couldn't hide my excitement to see her. She was dressed casually, so different from all the other women I had ever been interested in. Everything about her seemed natural and pure. I liked the simplicity in her beauty.

Her eyes were a brighter brown in the sunlight, so brown that I couldn't take my gaze off them as she walked down the porch to the sidewalk. I rushed to meet her and took her hands in mine. I loved the feel of her soft and delicate hand intertwined with my more masculine one. I wanted to kiss her, but I worried it would be too forward and too quick if I kept kissing her all the time like I wanted to. Something about Quinn made me want to take my time. My control, however, wasn't strong enough to fight off the urge to at least hug her, so I did, closely, intimately. I almost moaned, feeling her hair tickle my face, breathing in everything about her.

Grudgingly, I finally pulled away and let her go. I kept my hand still fastened to hers as I walked her to the car and opened the door for her.

Once I started the car and drove off, I found it impossible to keep my hands off her. We made small talk, but every chance I got, I caressed her leg, her arm, her face. I couldn't shake the feeling that she belonged to me. That I belonged to her. The connection and the bond pulled at me with a full-strength intensity. I couldn't fight the urge to bring Quinn's hand to my mouth and kiss it. I had no idea what was happening. This was unlike me to be so affectionate and so attentive. Could she possibly feel the same? I tried to control myself before I freaked her the fuck out by acting too intense, but I couldn't help my actions. The only saving grace was it didn't seem like Quinn minded, and at times, she even caressed my hand in return. She seemed to welcome my touch.

I was excited to take her someplace quiet and private, somewhere different than the clubs and bars. I wanted to talk to her, get to know more about her, more about this woman who overpowered my entire being. I wanted to get closer. I wanted more. For the first time in my life, I wanted Quinn and only Quinn. It was fast, impulsive, and downright crazy, but I knew she was special, and I didn't want to play around with the typical games. I knew it was risky acting too fast and pushing too much, but not riskier than denying the way I felt and letting her walk away.

I had packed a picnic lunch and planned to take her to a grassy park area overlooking the city skyline. I hoped she enjoyed the place as much as I did. I smiled when I looked over at her gazing out the window, admiring the amazing views.

"My God, this place is remarkable! You can see the entire city from here," she gushed.

I liked seeing her enthusiasm. No matter how many times I came up here, I always found it as awe-inspiring as the first time. I took a moment to admire the view before turning to her. The view didn't measure up to the beauty sitting next to me. She truly was the most attractive woman I had ever seen.

"I have a picnic for us. I thought we'd enjoy the peace and quiet."

Quinn's eyes widened a bit, but she smiled and got out of the car. We laid out the blanket and put down the basket. We both sat in silence, taking in the scenery. The silence didn't feel awkward at all, but rather calm and relaxing. Everything seemed so natural and comfortable that I couldn't hold back any longer. I leaned in for a small but sensual kiss. A kiss that was soft and sweet, but passionate at the same time. Pressing her back gently, laying her down on the blanket, I propped myself up on my elbow next to her. I positioned her body closer to mine while my hand caressed her body over her clothes. Every touch slow, making sure I didn't overstep.

I nibbled her lower lip softly, then worked my way down to her neck and the tip of her ear. I tasted, I licked, I relished the delightful scent of Quinn. Everything about her intoxicated my senses. I ran my hand over her stomach and then down her outer thigh. I had never felt more aroused, nor had any other woman ever made me want to take it further so badly.

"Axel," Quinn whispered, hoarsely.

I moaned softly as I continued to kiss and suckle her neck, wishing now we were somewhere where we could get more intimate. There was no one around, but I wasn't sure what Quinn's thoughts were on sex in public. But fuck I wanted her so bad!

"Axel." I could feel how hard she was breathing and was excited to see that she possibly wanted the same.

I kissed her with more fervor, dancing my tongue with hers. I kissed until our breaths united as one, merging a combined passion. Loving every moment, I pulled away so I could gaze into the depths of her eyes. Satisfied with the lust I saw swirling amongst the brown, I smiled.

"You're beautiful, Quinn." I ran small circles with my fingertip on her stomach as I spoke.

"Axel, there's something I need to tell you. I'm... well, I've never been..." Quinn took a deep breath and looked away from my locked stare. "I don't usually move this fast with men. I'm not the type that hooks up. I... fuck... I'm a virgin."

I stared at her blankly for a second, not sure how to respond. It felt as if the air had been knocked out of me. The idea of being Quinn's first experience rattled every nerve in my body. Confusion mixed with shock kept all the words locked inside. I wasn't sure what to say. Hell, I wasn't even sure what I thought. When I didn't respond immediately, Quinn sat up and pulled away from me.

"Wait, hold on..." I reached for her.

She turned to face me with tears glistening in her eyes. "I'm sorry. I know I should've said something."

I reached for her hands, my head spinning. "I'm confused. Have I been reading you wrong this whole time? I would never pressure you into something against your will. I would never make you have sex until you were ready. I had no idea you were saving yourself."

She looked embarrassed and bit her bottom lip, not making eye contact. "No, you haven't. I've been enjoying this. Enjoying you." She took a deep breath. "I'm not waiting for marriage or anything like that."

"So, you aren't saving yourself?"

Quinn shook her head. "No. I just usually go really slow. And then by the time I feel I'm ready for sex, the relationship has already crumbled. I guess I wait too long." She paused and reluctantly looked up to meet my eyes. "But with you… with you, I question my feelings about waiting. Maybe I'd like to try? I don't know. I'm confused."

"I thought you were more experienced. I've never met a virgin, especially in the club scene—"

"Felicity got me the job," she interrupted. "And yes, I know we are a rare breed. A fucked up breed." A tear escaped her eye. "I'm so sorry. I'm not leading you on, or messing with you. I swear. I'm just really god damn naïve. It's embarrassing."

"It's okay. Just relax." I caressed her cheek, wiping away the tear. "I'm sorry I came on so strong. I should have been more of a gentleman. I hope I'm not scaring you away."

"Don't apologize. I'm the one who should. I want you. I do. But then, I'm freaking the fuck out too."

I put my arm around her and kissed her head. "We don't have to figure this out overnight. Do you want to explore this? See where this goes? Take the time that is needed?"

"Do you?" she asked softly.

"Yes, very much."

"What if I'm just fucked up? What if I drag this out until it takes too long and you get tired of waiting? What if I overthink this shit like I did every other time?"

I frowned against the soft hair of her head. I pulled her closer and kissed the top of her head again. "Do you want to stop what's happening between us? Is this too much for you?" My body tensed as I waited for the answer.

"No. I don't want this to stop at all." Quinn snuggled her head under my chin, wrapping her arms around my chest. "Can you be patient with me? Help me through all of this?"

I squeezed her tight. "Yes, I can. I will."

She looked up at me and smiled. "All I know is, this feels right. You feel right."

I loved seeing her smile. "I agree. I'll be here for you every step of the way. I want there to be an 'us.' But if this ever feels wrong—"

"I can't imagine that," she interrupted again.

"Then we'll figure this out. We'll make it work."

* * * * *

Quinn

I sat across from Axel, eating my sandwich and admiring every move he made. Even the way he ate was sexy. I still couldn't believe how understanding he was about the whole virgin issue. He wasn't acting like I was some freak of nature. His calm demeanor, sensitivity, and compassion caused me to care about him even more. I was falling for him, falling like I had never done before.

The sound of my ringing phone interrupted my thoughts. "Oh, sorry," I said as I scrambled to find my phone to dismiss the call.

Axel shook his head, wiping off his mouth. "No worries. Go ahead and answer it."

I looked down at the caller ID. "It's my friend, Harrison. I'll just let it go to voicemail."

Axel shrugged. "Go ahead and talk to him." He smiled. "He could be calling for something important. I don't mind at all."

I felt my stomach stir. For some reason, I didn't like the idea of talking to my editor in front of him.

I knew Axel had no idea who Harrison really was, but it felt wrong. My head still spun from the conversation we'd just had and my feelings about Axel. I'd never been a liar in my life, and leading Axel to believe Harrison was only a friend was technically lying. Although I could also reason with myself that I'd never actually *said* Harrison wasn't an editor and I wasn't a writer. I should tell Axel; it really wasn't a big deal. I really should—but I couldn't. I had already just dropped a bombshell. The virgin bombshell should be enough. One confession at a time.

"No," I said, a little too hastily. "I can call when I get home." I leaned in and gave a quick peck to his lips. "I want to spend time with you. No interruptions."

"Come closer." Axel opened his arms, smiling. "Let me hold you."

I moved into his embrace, cozying up to his warmth.

"Quinn, I hope this doesn't sound too insane, but I really like you." He reached for one of my hands and started to kiss my fingertips, one at a time. "I know I just met you, but I feel like I could spend every day and every moment with you... if you'd let me."

I gazed up into his eyes, swallowing the lump in the back of my throat. My heart pounded and butterflies danced in my stomach. "I know what you mean," I whispered.

"I know you said you're only going to be here a short while. And I know the fact that I live a pretty fucked up life is an issue. But I was hoping... I was hoping we could continue to spend time together."

"Really?" I giggled. I felt like I was a love-struck teenager. "Are you asking me to be your girlfriend?" I teased. I joked, but there was a wishful thinking element to my comment.

Axel cleared his throat, obviously uncomfortable. "Well, yes. I mean, if the idea doesn't scare you off." He pulled me in closer. "I'm not good at stuff like this. There really is no easy way to broach this subject without sounding so cheesy. All I know is that I want you and me to be together... solely. At least while you're here."

I sat in silence, overwhelmed by the realization that I was about to become the girlfriend of Axel Rye, the man I had come to secretly get information on for my book. My stomach did flips as I tried to take it all in. Could I have a boyfriend and a book deal?

My emotions jumbled: I was happy, ecstatic, scared, shocked, and timid. I turned to him with a serious expression. "What if I can't buy into this whole drug thing? I still haven't wrapped my head around working in a club every night let alone dating someone who represents it. I mean, what do I tell my parents? What do I tell them about you? If you are my boyfriend, I sort of have to tell them about you." Oh my God, I sounded like a little girl.

I saw his eyes narrow while he looked at me skeptically. "Well, the fact of the matter is I am what I am. You have to be comfortable with that. One Google search and everyone will know—including your parents—what I do for a living. I don't believe in keeping secrets." He paused. "But why don't we agree to not make this about defining. Let's make this about two people who have feelings for each other, and take it from there." He chuckled. "No need getting the parental figures involved on either end. Trust me, you do not want to meet mine."

"They can't be that bad."

"Oh they are. Really bad. Dear old Dad is in Europe someplace banging girls half his age while he tries to hold onto his youth. My mother… hell, I have no idea what she is up to. I haven't spoken to either in a couple of years."

I tilted my head in confusion. "But your court case. Weren't they there?"

"Oh hell no. Are you kidding me? They didn't want the shame to wreak havoc on their perfect little worlds." He sighed. "Enough talk about my parents. That is the most I have thought about them in ages, and I feel I need to pop a Valium and pay for therapy sessions by just doing so."

"I'm sorry to bring it up. Nothing for killing the mood like talking about parents," I said with a giggle.

"I don't mind. Some day we will have to deal with them. But not today. Today, I want to talk only about you and me and us."

"Us," I mimicked.

He nodded. "Us."

"And your lifestyle? Do I really fit in with that? You're famous, and every woman at these hot spots would die to be with you. I'm not exactly the exciting girlfriend type. I may kill your vibe."

"It's a job. I would never betray you because of a paycheck." He was firm. "My friends will love you because you're an amazing person. As for the fame, we'll muddle through it. It's a pain. I'm not going to lie. But I want you to be with me."

Grinning from ear to ear, I wrapped my arms around Axel's neck. "I would love to be your girlfriend!" I kissed him and pulled away quickly. "I love it!"

Axel stared at me, expressionless, for an instant. Then, as if he suddenly comprehended what I just agreed to, his grin matched mine. He put his hand behind my neck, pulling me closer, pressing my lips hard against his own. Our lips brushed and tested as we explored the growing connection between us. The touch of our lips was soft, unsure of what was to come. This kiss seemed as if our souls combined. I took in Axel's breath, as he took in mine. We paused and took a moment to look into each other's eyes. I could feel the kiss in the depths of my heart. I could feel the most wonderful moment of my life.

Axel groaned. I muffled the sound and tangled my tongue with his, kissing him with all the passion that exploded from within, until I panted for more, until our bodies strained together and everything disappeared but the ravenous quest of our mouths.

The hard, warm weight of Axel pressed against me, one hand slipping inside my loose blouse and behind me to trace the low curve of my spine, then ever so gently lower, to the top of my bottom, where his caress slid the material of my skirt in sinuous circles against my hyper-sensitive flesh.

Panting, struggling for breath, I broke the kiss to stare into his perfect face. I had to touch him, to feel him. I spread my fingers over the rugged surface of his cheek, moving them down to the firmness of his moistened lips. Axel was the most handsome man I had ever seen.

Not quite brave enough, suddenly, to meet his eyes, I leaned my forehead against his throat, tugged the white shirt from his jeans and slipped my hand under its hem to find Axel's firm abdomen and the softness of his bare skin. I felt a sense of triumph at the quiver of his stomach muscles and the near-silent sound of desperation that escaped his lips.

Axel sucked in a breath as my touch moved around his waist to his spine, where I flattened my palm against the smoothness of his back and let my fingertips slip over every muscled hill and valley.

With a moan, Axel jerked my hand from beneath his shirt and drew it to his lips, kissing each finger before he released a shaky sigh. "Don't get me wrong, I love what you're doing. But if we don't stop…"

"If we don't stop…" I echoed in a haze, watching Axel's lips move against my hand and wanting them on my mouth instead.

"I'm going to take you right here. I have very little self-control."

That prospect didn't sound half bad to me, but suddenly we heard voices and a dog barking, and the sound hovered all around us. The spell was broken.

Embarrassment heated my cheeks, both from being more aggressive than I had ever been and from my public displays of affection. I would have had sex with Axel right then and there if it weren't for the damn dog. Fuck being a virgin. "This isn't like me at all. But there's something about you—"

"There's something about us," Axel interrupted softly. "Why don't we take a break? I think I should probably take you home… for now. Otherwise it's going to be pretty hard to respect that virgin card of yours."

The drive to Felicity's apartment was quieter than I would have liked. I met Axel's gaze several times during the drive. He had the most alluring eyes. With each look, the fire blazed between us.

I reached over and touched his cheek. "Thank you," I said. "For being understanding with me."

"I've never been good with this whole courting thing." Axel blew out a breath, thrust his fingers through his disheveled hair, and cast me an enticing smile. "You make me feel… different. You make me want to be a better man." He let out a low laugh. "Just don't tell anyone that. I have a reputation."

At the front door of the apartment, I stopped and turned to face Axel. "I had a really nice time." He gave an easy nod, his brown-eyed gaze scanning my face. "It was fun," I added. "Well, not fun, exactly. More like... a million other physical sensations. I've never felt this way before. It's so confusing, but in a good way. Does that make any sense?"

Axel laughed and stepped closer to me, slid a hand beneath my hair, and pressed his lips to my forehead. When he spoke, his voice was a husky rumble that seared me to the bone. "I know exactly how you feel."

"I don't want you to leave," I admitted. I fiddled with the simple silver chain around his neck, staring at the satiny skin beneath it. "I have a feeling things are going to move quickly between us."

"That's completely up to you. I have the same feeling, but I don't want to make you do anything you are uncomfortable with. Agreeing to fully give yourself to me is a huge step. I don't take the matter lightly. When you do, is something I'm going to allow you to dictate. My libido may disagree, but I want this to be all you."

A faint smile tugged at my mouth, and I glanced up at Axel through my lashes. "How I feel right now… things are going to move quickly. My libido is in cahoots with yours."

"You better go inside," Axel whispered intensely. "Before I change my mind about letting you have the control."

Filled with a feminine power I'd never experienced, I tugged him against me and caught his mouth in a long-lasting, blazing kiss. "Goodbye, Axel."

Chapter 6

All To Fucking See

Quinn

It was almost implausible to me what a whirlwind of emotions the past few days had been. Coming to terms with my feelings, my sexual desires, and my choice to be with Axel made my head spin.

I had told Harrison everything that had happened, and that Axel and I were more than just friends or a means to a book deal. Although shocked at first, Harrison laughed and teased me about being in love. He warned me to take it slow and remain somewhat guarded, but also encouraged me to explore my feelings about the possibility of being in a relationship. He also had informed me that I was not allowed to give up on the book deal.

That this was my life, my future, and I had a career to think about. A lustful encounter with Axel Rye was not worth giving up everything for.

I almost jumped for joy when I heard my phone ring and saw Axel's name on the screen. I answered it with a huge smile and tried to hide a squeal that threatened to escape my lips. This was ridiculous. Truly ridiculous.

"Hi, Axel."

"Hey." His voice sounded soft, seductive. "Sorry I'm calling so late. My night went later than I thought. I couldn't stop thinking about us. I honestly don't like being apart from you."

"I feel exactly the same." I clutched the phone, as if it were his hand. Cheesy yes, but it's still what I did. "I feel like I'm walking on air. I'm really happy." I hoped I didn't seem too honest, but I didn't want to hold back how much I liked him. I sucked at game playing anyway.

"I'm really happy, too," he said. "It's almost scary how happy I am right now."

I sat down on my bed. "I'm glad you called. I wanted to talk about your career."

"My career? Last I checked, I didn't exactly have a career."

"Okay, maybe not a career exactly, but you're famous. How's it going to look if you're dating someone? Won't it cramp your style? Isn't your playboy lifestyle part of what makes you cool?"

Axel laughed. "Cramp my style? No, it won't, and I don't care if it does."

"What about if it gets out that I'm just a boring girl next door? No fame, no glitz and glamour. You're in demand at every club, bar, and big event. You don't think it will make you look... fake?"

Axel was silent for a moment. "I'm genuine. Everything I do is honest. I put myself out there. If people don't like that, I really don't care. I'm not going to change the way I act, the decisions I make, or my feelings for you, because of this bizarre notoriety. I'm not going to pretend I'm single because of an image I should uphold."

"I just don't want to get in the way of what you do. I understand what you do for a living—"

"It's a job, and only a job. I'm not going to let it get in the way of us. Understood?"

The truth was I wasn't entirely sure I could handle this. I knew how other women, especially Jillian and Axel's groupies, acted around Axel. The thought of watching other girls throw themselves all over him made me sick to my stomach.

I took a calming breath. "Understood."

"In case there's any doubt, I wasn't planning on keeping you a secret. I'm going to be proud to have you on my arm."

I felt my pulse speed up. The reality of it all started to sink in. This was really happening. I was the girlfriend of the famous Axel Rye. "Okay. I just want you to know I'm not that needy girl. I can let you be in the spotlight but still be there when you're all done."

"That's not what I want," he said. "If anyone is going to be that *needy person*, it's going to be me.

In case you haven't noticed, I just can't get enough of you."

Axel's words sent a wave of warmth through my body. I felt the exact same way, although Axel didn't seem frightened by it. I, on the other hand, was petrified. This seemed too good to be true.

"You have to stop melting my heart," I whispered.

"Why?" Axel suddenly sounded serious. "I say what I feel, and I want you to always do the same. Don't ever hold anything back. Honesty is all we have. We need to be free with what we feel."

"Okay." I loved how Axel made me feel so open, and I wasn't going to think about the book deal and let it ruin this moment. I couldn't. I just couldn't. "Can I tell you what I'm feeling right now?"

"Always."

I took a deep breath and nibbled at my bottom lip. "I want to be with you right now, and kiss you all over."

I heard Axel's breath hitch. "You're making it very hard for me not to hop in my car, pick you up, and keep you with me always."

I giggled. "Sweet dreams, Axel."

"My dreams will be of you."

I held the phone to my heart for a while after we'd hung up and wondered how I could go another moment without Axel in my life.

* * * * *

Quinn

True to his word, Axel didn't keep our relationship a secret. As soon as he saw me at work, Axel was all over me. He walked behind the bar and wrapped his arms around my waist, kissing my neck.

Axel obviously felt comfortable with his dominance and power. He knew he could pretty much do anything at this club, and he had no problem showing affection to me. Axel didn't hold back a thing. He could hardly keep his hands off my body.

"Axel, my boss isn't going to like you behind here. I need to finish my shift before you get me fired."

"Your boss isn't going to say a thing, and you know it."

I playfully tried to push him away. "You are so bad. Do rules not apply to you?"

"I don't like sharing you. I'm selfish. I want you all to myself," Axel explained, intertwining his fingers with mine. "Is it quitting time yet?"

"I thought you had a job to do? Aren't you supposed to be mingling with all the club-goers and getting them to buy off you?" I inquired somewhat timidly. I hoped Axel enjoyed our flirtations as much as I did, but I did hate mentioning him dealing drugs. But I also knew it was part of his life and I needed to get used to it.

"I'm mingling with the *staff*. Much more than I ever have before," Axel declared, glancing up at me suggestively as he continued playing with my hand behind the bar. I couldn't help but smile at that as I looked up from our restless hands to gaze at Axel flirtatiously. I felt a shudder run through me when I saw the predatory look in his eyes.

"I should probably get back to work," I said softly, reluctantly pulling my hand away from Axel's. I needed to focus my attention back to pouring drinks before I slid under the counter out of view of others and did something decidedly inappropriate at work.

"Aren't you done yet?" Axel whined, and I half-expected him to start pouting like a little boy. An incredibly sexy little boy.

"Soon," I replied. Axel reached out and took my hand again, using his index finger to lightly trace patterns along my palm. "And then I'm all yours."

"Can't you just clock out early?" Axel suggested, sticking out his lower lip petulantly.

How was it possible for anyone to look so adorable and deliciously dangerous at the same time? "I can pay you and the club whatever amount. I just want you now." He had a mischievous glint to his eye, and I simply could not deny him anything with how cute he looked.

"I guess I could clock out," I conceded. "I'm not of much help right now, anyway." For some reason, I found it impossible to say no to Axel.

"Good," Axel said, interrupting my wayward thoughts. "Because I want to introduce you to some more of my friends."

"I thought you wanted me all to yourself?" I asked in confusion.

Axel followed me to the back room with a dominant presence, causing my heart to skip a beat. He slowly walked over to me and tugged me softly into his arms. He pulled away and placed a palm of his hand on each side of my face. Very closely, he examined my eyes. "I do," Axel admitted, and I eyed him suspiciously as we walked to the timecard machine. "But I also want everyone to know you belong to me."

"Are you sure? You don't have to do that," I asked, nervously licking my lips as I clocked out and took off my apron.

"Yes, I do," he stated, reaching out to run his finger down the length of my arm. "I want everyone to know I've fallen hard."

"Fallen?" I asked anxiously.

He leaned forward and pressed his lips against mine, effectively shutting me up. The kiss was chaste, less intimate than the gentle exploration of mouths we had exchanged the day before. Axel's lips ruthlessly stroked my own, sending little jolts of pleasure through my body. I kissed him back, my lips parting slightly as I sighed in contentment. Kissing Axel Rye was quickly becoming a habit I had no intention of ever giving up. I moaned softly when I felt Axel's tongue gently lapping at my lower lip, demanding entrance. Opening my mouth a bit wider, I eagerly anticipated the feel of Axel's tongue slipping past my lips and into the warm confines of my mouth. But instead of deepening the kiss, Axel ended it. With one last gentle nip to my lower lip, he pulled back slightly, looking entirely too pleased with himself when I groaned in protest.

"Yes. Fallen," he answered, his voice taking on a seductive quality that made my stomach do a little flip flop.

"Oh, yeah." I sighed, grinning at him in satisfaction. "But just let the record show that technically, I've *fallen* harder."

"Sounds like someone has a bit of a competitive streak," Axel teased, returning my smile.

"I do. You should know that I never lose," I replied confidently. I immensely enjoyed this little game and flirtation of ours. But I knew I needed to cool things down or I would demand for him to take me right then and there. But was that really a bad thing? Maybe not every girl's dream was getting fucked and losing her virginity in the break room, but I was at the point of not caring anymore on how it happened. I was far past roses and soft words of endearment. Accepting his lifestyle still confused me. Even more so now that my feelings grew stronger by the moment, but one thing was very clear: I wanted Axel.

"Well then, maybe I should give you a challenge." Axel leered at me suggestively, leaning in for another kiss.

I closed my eyes for a moment, searching my entire being for the courage for what I was about to do. "Challenge accepted." I paused. "I want this moment. I want this moment to feel you." I tentatively pressed my palm to his chest. "I want this moment to taste you." I lowered my hand to the bulge in Axel's pants. "I want this moment to feel your cock between my lips." I quickly undid his zipper and button releasing his thickness from his confines. For the first time in my life, I allowed my passion to rule over my mind. I couldn't believe I'd actually said the word "cock" out loud. Something was changing in me. Something was awakening.

Axel stood still, never making a move to stop me in my mission. I took this as a sign to continue on. I knelt down and softly placed his hardened cock on the base of my tongue and closed my lips tightly around him. Looking up into his eyes, I began to move my mouth up and down along his shaft. He never looked away. He never closed his eyes for a moment. He watched as I began my seduction. I tightened my lips, and worked my tongue in small circles along the entire length. His taste, his smell, and his delicious aura were everything I had imagined.

Axel reached for my hair to stop me. "Quinn," he moaned.

I looked up into his eyes with his cock still in my mouth. I pulled it out enough to whisper, "Don't, Axel. I'm not the innocent, naïve girl you see. I am a woman with desires, needs, and a hunger for you like nothing I could have imagined." I lowered my mouth down to the base of his cock and slowly back to the tip. Removing his penis just enough to speak again, I rasped, "Let me pleasure you."

Axel closed his eyes and threw his head back in euphoric surrender. I knew I had won this battle. I smiled wickedly at my success and continued my quest to please him like he had never experienced before. I wanted to show all those groupies before me a thing or two.

Suddenly the break-room door opened with a gust of loud music pouring in. A woman in a black dress and even blacker hair engulfing her pale face stood in the doorway. Dilated eyes were almost hidden by even darker circles underneath them. Scarlet lips worked their way into a smirk as she crossed her arms across her ample breasts.

"Oh, don't mind me. Please continue on," she offered with the most seductive voice I had ever heard.

Axel pulled away. "Jillian, what the fuck are you doing?"

I scrambled to my feet in shock and embarrassment as Axel quickly adjusted his pants.

"Well, obviously not nearly having as much fun as you. My, my, Axel. Just when I thought you were getting boring. Public play... I like. Care to share?"

"Get out of here," Axel demanded as he marched toward the door.

The biting command stung me to the core. I had never heard Axel talk with such a demanding voice before. I had never seen Axel lose control of his temper like I saw now. Obviously, the woman had a negative effect on him.

"Don't get mad, Axel. Well, unless you want to spank my naughty bottom," Jillian giggled as she seductively licked her lips.

I stiffened my spine.

Axel moved with lightning speed until he glared down at Jillian's small frame. "I said get out! I'm not in the mood for your fucked up junkie games." Axel ushered Jillian out, slamming the door behind her, and turned to me. "I'm so sorry. When Jillian is high… well actually, that's just Jillian. I'm sorry if she embarrassed you."

I forced a fake smile. "It's okay."

"No, it's not. But I don't want to think about that crazy bitch anymore."

I looked into his deep eyes and said nothing. I met his gaze and allowed for him to truly see my embarrassment of being caught in such an intimate act. When it came to this man, I had no reason to hide my feelings.

Axel pulled me into his arms harshly. He pressed my head to his chest with more force than I had ever experienced. "I won't let it happen again. I'll make sure I protect you from all the insanity of my life. I never want to be the cause of your heartache." Without releasing his grip, he continued, "But I have to warn you that my image as this party bad boy tends to attract the mentally unstable people at times. I swear to you my loyalty, but being with me can be really hard on trust."

I pulled from his strong embrace. "I trust you, Axel. I know you'd never hurt me." I smiled. "Weren't you going to introduce me to your friends?" I reminded him, leaning away from him as I grabbed my purse from the locker and prepared to leave.

"Don't I at least get a kiss to hold me off?" Axel teased.

"Nope," I replied casually, offering him a playful wink.

"Why not?" he complained, his puppy dog eyes pleading with me to stay.

Seductively, I wrapped my arms around Axel's neck and moved my mouth until it was pressed up against his ear. "Because the next time you kiss me, I won't want you to stop," I whispered, feeling him shudder as my warm breath tickled his earlobe. And with that, I led Axel over to join his friends.

Hanging out in the VIP section with an unlimited amount of booze and drugs was a whole new experience. Everyone watched and examined our every move. It was like being inside a fish bowl. The curiosity about this new girl with Axel caused quite the stir, although Axel didn't seem affected by all the attention in the slightest.

"Help yourself," Teddy said to me as he passed a mirror with lines of white powder. He handed me a rolled up hundred dollar bill as if I had done this a million times. I hadn't, and really had no idea what to do.

I paused just enough for Knox to take the glass out of my hand. "Don't mind if I do." He put the rolled up bill to one nostril, closed the other nostril with his finger, and then snorted hard as he ran the rolled tube along the white line. I watched in fascination as he then sat up, leaned his head back and sniffed hard. His white line was completely gone.

He then passed the mirror to me, with the rolled money. "Sorry, I skipped in line. All yours."

I took the mirror again, and the money and mimicked exactly as he did, not noticing—or trying not to notice—that Axel was watching me intently. I knew if I looked at Axel, I would get nervous and mess it all up. I didn't want to seem like a sweet, innocent girl from the burbs. I wanted to fit in with this crowd so bad. I wanted to prove to Axel that I could be like all of them.

And just like that, I snorted coke. Or I assumed it was coke.

Axel didn't say anything, and acted as if nothing happened. He took the mirror from me and took his turn with another line. It was as simple as passing a bottle of water on a hot day. Completely normal in their world. He then leaned in and kissed me hard, wrapping his arm around me as we chatted with the group.

We were undeniably a couple. We received a few dirty looks and heard whispered comments from Axel's groupies, but if Axel noticed, he didn't say a word. I had expected him to be somewhat tense or cautious in showing affection. But his blatant show of attention made it very clear to all that I was his girl. The way Axel acted and carried himself throughout the night made me fall for him even more… if that was even possible.

Although Axel's friends seemed surprised, they didn't say much. Knox just smiled and made a point to include me in conversation. Teddy also did his part in welcoming me to the group.

By the end of the night, it was out there for everyone to see. Axel and I were inseparable.

Chapter 7

Best Fucking Gift

Quinn

After a few weeks, we had slipped into a comfortable routine. I would work behind the bar while Axel worked the room with his friends. We'd always meet afterwards to hang out there or at whatever club requested Axel to appear that night. We would then go grab something to eat and indulge in some much-needed alone time. I was becoming quite the night owl, and loving every minute of it. Drugs were becoming part of my nightly routine, but it was hard not to. Keeping up with the vampire hours, as Axel liked to call them, usually required a quick line, or a little pill. I didn't mind really. I had Axel looking over me, and I felt safe and protected. I was letting loose as everyone once told me I needed to do. I was living life and as far outside my safe little white box as one could get.

Everything between us was going perfectly, except for a couple of incidents with Jillian. She had made it a point to flirt with Axel as often as she got the chance. I had seen the displays, but chose to ignore it. Axel didn't feed into it and, at times, seemed oblivious to Jillian throwing herself on him. The rest of the girls tossing their barely-clad bodies on him were even more pathetic. I found it annoying at times, but harmless.

All that mattered at this point was that Axel and I were solid. I felt happier than I ever had, and I actually looked forward to the future, as uncertain as it was. Nothing could bring me down from the high I felt. Life with Axel was beyond anything I could have pictured. Happiness wasn't a strong enough word.

* * * * *

Axel

I had a photo shoot for a new Indie magazine, a restaurant appearance, and then a bar's grand opening to attend. I had agreed to meet Quinn afterwards at her work and pick her up at the end of her shift. All I wanted was to be alone with her and have some peace and quiet, but I still had a job—or jobs—to do. The night's schedule was a true test in time management.

I walked into the club with Teddy and Knox, looking around for Quinn. We had run behind schedule, and I hoped I hadn't kept her waiting for too long. I spotted Felicity first, and then I saw Quinn. There were a few guys talking to them, causing me to suddenly tense up. The feeling was ridiculous since I knew Quinn was mine, but seeing her talk to a man sent a sickening feeling to my gut. It was just another reason I was so over this club scene. This wasn't what I wanted for Quinn. She deserved so much better. I walked straight to her and took her hand immediately, hating the jealousy that racked my body. Pulling her away from everyone, I kissed her. To my delight, she didn't resist. She kissed me readily and with passion.

"I've missed you." She smiled against my kiss.

I pulled back and stared at her, holding her tighter. "You're beautiful. Walking into this club, I realized you are the most stunning woman in this room." I kissed the top of her head. "But then that happens every time I walk into a room."

"There you go, melting my heart again." She tilted her head sideways. Rising on her tiptoes, she whispered in my ear, "Do you want to get out of here, or do you think you need to stay for a while?"

"I'm not getting paid to be here tonight. So, yes, I want to be alone with you." I pulled her even closer.

We barely made it to my car before we started caressing, kissing, driving each other crazy with each touch. The passion between us grew heavier and heavier every day that passed. I had been patient and tried to take things slow. I didn't want to scare Quinn, or make her doubt her relationship with me. I was dying to take it to the next level, but wanted to leave that in her hands like I promised. On the surface, it appeared she felt comfortable with everything, but I knew she struggled with her sexual thoughts. The first time was a big deal and needed to be done right. I didn't want it to be a "drunken or high naughty experiment." If we were to make love, I wanted it to be just that: making love. And sadly, as much as I hated to admit it, we had been high a lot lately.

When we got to my loft, Quinn sat down on the leather couch, gazing at the city lights out the bay window. Her hair, illuminated by the moonlight, captured my soul. I felt like the air had been knocked out of me. She almost appeared angelic.

"I'll get us some wine," I offered as I walked to the kitchen to pour the glasses.

"I really love your place. This view makes me never want to leave." Quinn turned to watch me pour the wine. "*You* make me never want to leave."

I walked over to where she sat and handed her the glass. "Then don't. I don't want you to."

We both sat there in silence for a moment, taking in the words I had just spoken. Neither of us wanted to broach the subject lingering between us since we started dating. When was Quinn leaving? Would she still leave? Would she ever really give herself to me? Was it realistic to think she could?

"Have I told you yet how incredibly beautiful you are tonight?"

Quinn giggled. "You tell it to me all the time." She leaned forward and kissed my parted lips, slipping her tongue gently into the warmth of my mouth.

I danced my tongue with hers, escalating the kiss to a higher level of need. My hands explored every inch of her, only to be rewarded by her following suit. I kissed her harder, suckling her tongue and lips. She moaned softly, driving my desire to an uncontrollable breaking point. Not being able to stop at just a kiss, as we had been doing up until now, I unbuttoned her blouse, one button at a time. Once I'd exposed her, I tenderly took Quinn's breast into my mouth.

My hand made its way slowly down Quinn's body, caressing her stomach, gently and slowly. Taking my time, even though I wanted to rip her clothes off and ravish her body with fury. With a controlled hand, I lowered my fingertips to the button on her pants and undid it gracefully.

My heart battered away uncontrollably as I passionately kissed her. Dipping my hand beneath the edge of her panties, I paused as she tensed. "Do you want me to stop?"

Quinn simply shook her head.

I continued to move my hand deeper beneath the fabric. When I felt the hot flesh against my fingertips, I couldn't help but softly moan. I wanted her more than I had ever wanted someone before.

Weeks of foreplay had truly tested my limits. I pulled my mouth away from the constant kissing to catch my breath, burying my face in the crook of Quinn's neck.

"God, I want you," I groaned as I inhaled the delicate scent that drove me crazy.

Quinn moved her hand cautiously over my chest, pausing for a moment, only to continue on. She slipped her hand beneath the cotton of my shirt, exploring along my burning flesh. Slowly, she slid her hand further down my torso, stopping at the edge of my pants. Quinn paused, appearing to hold her breath.

I looked into her eyes. "Are you okay?"

She spread her legs while nodding, causing my heart to skip. "Quinn" was the only word I could gasp, as I lowered her pants to gain better access.

I pulled back to look into her smoldering eyes, knowing that if I kept going, I wouldn't want to stop. "I want you so much. But if you're not ready, I understand. I want this to be right for you." I could barely catch my breath, my hunger unbearable.

* * * * *

Quinn

I threaded my fingers through Axel's hair, tugging on his locks enough to bring our lips into full, open contact. Diving my tongue deep into his kiss, I moaned, "I want this. I want you."

Suddenly Axel stood up, his eyes dark and scorching with need. He met my gaze as he removed his clothing, never breaking the stare. Standing before me naked, he slowly bent down to kiss me once again. With slow and deliberate movements, Axel removed my clothes the remainder of the way.

I drew in a breath, my eyes still locked with Axel's, almost frightened to look away.

He caressed my face. "I'm falling in love with you, Quinn. I would never hurt you, and I don't want to scare you." He continued to stare while caressing my cheek with the most tender of touches. "But I want you to truly give yourself to me. I want this to be your first real experience of making love."

I broke the stare to gaze at Axel's delicious body. His muscular chest, his body taut with animalistic need. I found my own body responding with a surge of desire. He was absolutely stunning, nude before me.

"I'm falling in love with you, too." My hands slipped down to his hips and drew him in even closer. "I want to give my virginity to you. I want you to show me how. Make me yours."

Axel leaned towards me to kiss me again, slipping his tongue past my lips and into my mouth. The hot breath caressed a fiery need in my core as a dark flame of passion burned between us. He wrapped me tighter in his arms, moving his lips to the side of my neck. I shivered as my body made

closer contact with Axel's nakedness. This was it…
we were about to make love. I was about to be fully
intimate and finally have sex.

Feeling Axel's chest pressed up against my own,
so warm, so soft, made me want to melt into the
embrace. I allowed my hands to drift experimentally
to Axel's cock. I caressed the smooth skin, feeling
almost dizzy with the new sensual feelings
pounding in me. Axel murmured his encouragement
and approval, which strengthened my courage to
continue.

"You're so hard," I moaned as I pressed small
kisses across his chest, while stroking his sex.

Axel pressed his lips hard against mine, his kiss
deep and full of passion. His tongue moved around
mine with a wave of wild heat. I could feel his
hardness pressing against me. I craved to get closer.
I wanted to see and feel all of him. As if Axel read
my mind, he swooped me up into his arms and
carried me to his bedroom.

He carried me to the bed and laid me back softly on the pillow. He kissed me gently and took a deep breath before speaking. "Is this what you want? Because Quinn, once we take this step, there is no turning back for us. You'll be mine, completely."

I could barely speak. "Yes, Axel. I want you. I do."

He cupped my breast and slowly lowered his mouth to my nipple. He sucked hard and began to nibble his way back to my neck, and when he reached the soft and sensitive skin below my ear, he sank his teeth in. I moaned in pleasure, feeling the heat radiate from between my legs.

"Oh, Axel!"

"God, this feels so right."

My eyes were drawn to his cock as he kneeled before me. He was big and hard and absolutely stunning. I licked my lips imagining his cock pumping in and out of my mouth. He moved closer to the bed as I positioned my body to take him in my mouth. Axel grasped the back of my head and guided his cock past my lips. He groaned when I flicked my tongue against the tip of his penis. I slid my mouth up and down his length, taking more of him each time. I circled my tongue around the tip, licking up the pre-cum. Slow and easy, I took him deeper.

With a groan, Axel thrust his cock to the back of my throat. "Yes, Quinn, like that. Take all of me."

I used my hand to stroke the length of his shaft as my mouth worked the head. I increased the suction, pulling him deeper. He began to thrust against my mouth, driving himself deeper with each pumping motion of his hips. I could feel his body tense with each touch of my tongue, anticipating his fluid, but suddenly Axel pulled my head back to look deep into my eyes.

"Jesus, you feel good." He pushed me back onto the bed. "You know how to drive me crazy."

Axel paused and his gaze fell to my exposed pussy. "I love how your pussy is bare, so smooth. I want you to always keep it this way," Axel lovingly commanded.

He gradually slipped his fingers into the soft folds of my pussy, then to my clit. He began to move one finger in a circular motion. I moaned and lifted, arching toward him in a silent plea for more. Axel lowered his head, burying it between my thighs. I screamed out his name when his mouth suddenly covered my clit. He leisurely drew it into his mouth and moved his tongue in long sensual strokes. I tightcned and twisted my body, fighting the wave of sensations overtaking me.

"Relax, Quinn. Don't fight it. It's just you and me, forever."

I felt the growing pleasure build in my body. He spread my velvety folds further and plunged his tongue deep inside, moving it in and out in a rhythmic pattern. I was hot and wet and ready to burst. His fingers played around my moist entrance before moving between the cheeks of my ass. I tensed as his finger applied pressure to my tight, puckered rosebud.

"Has anyone ever taken you here before?" Axel asked with a deep seductive voice.

I shook my head and could barely whisper, "No."

Axel growled as he pressed his index finger past the tight ring. I bucked against him. The width of his finger invading my ass sent a sensation of pleasure and pain that had me on the verge of climax. He sank his finger in deeper while using his other hand to rub my clit.

"I will, Quinn. Not tonight, but soon. I want to get you used to the feeling, and get you ready to accept me. I will have all of you. I will fuck this ass, just as I will fuck your pussy tonight," Axel said before gently pumping his finger in and out of my tight entrance.

Unexpectedly, Axel pulled away, and I felt him spread my legs further apart. Axel devoured my mouth in a breathless kiss as he pressed his bulging cock against my dripping wet pussy. Axel placed a hand on each side of my face, looking deep into my eyes. Never looking away, he slowly eased his hard cock into my welcoming pussy. There was a pop and I cried out, but I didn't want him to stop. It hurt, but not so badly that it overcame my need for more.

He paused for a moment, giving me the time I needed to adjust to the sensation that he was inside of me. That I was no longer a virgin, and he had broken the barrier. When I kissed his neck, he took the cue I was ready for more, and began to gently move. I wanted it all. He thrust in and out, never taking his eyes away from mine. He was so deep, rocking forward, deeper than I thought possible.

I could feel my sex clench around his cock. My inner muscles pulsated as I pressed into his every thrust. My heart thumped out of control. I gasped for breath as he began to press his cock deeper and faster. He slipped his hand behind my head, his fingers tangled in the strands and pulled. The sharp pain only added to my pleasure, pulling me towards orgasm. I felt a building of pleasure unlike anything I had known. This sensation was a far cry from masturbation. I dug my nails into Axel's back, and I began to scream as my body reached the ultimate orgasm. It hurt so bad, yet it felt so good.

Axel pressed deeper, harder, and faster, his cock possessing my depths. I felt his body tense and his breathing become ragged. His pace quickened, causing me to have another fiery sensation course through my body. I screamed out his name as his body stiffened and his warm release filled me.

He settled his mouth over mine, kissing me slowly. I enjoyed his tenderness as we relaxed in the aftermath of the best sex I could ever imagine by far. Axel rolled to the side and let out a huge breath.

"God! That was fucking amazing." He put his arms around me and pulled me close so I could rest my head on his chest. "I have never experienced anything like that. You're absolutely incredible. Thank you for giving me such a special gift." He kissed the top of my head. "I love you, Quinn."

I closed my eyes. "I love you with all my heart, Axel." And I fell asleep to the beating of his heart, no longer the woman I once was.

Chapter 8

Love Fucking Surprises

Quinn

I woke to the welcoming scent of freshly brewed coffee. My body was still delightfully sore in places I wasn't aware were capable of ever being sore. Axel and I had spent hours making love into the night, neither of us able to get enough. Slowly rolling to my back and stretching my body, I smiled at the amazing memories flooding in. Checking the time on my phone on the bedside table, I was surprised to see I had slept so late. I quickly got out of bed, pulled on one of Axel's t-shirts, and made my way into the kitchen.

"Good morning, beautiful." Axel walked over and placed a mug of coffee in my hands as he leaned down to brush a kiss on my forehead.

"If you keep this up, you're going to spoil me so much that you'll never be able to get rid of me."

"Well, maybe that's my plan." He winked at me as he bent his head, bunched his fist into my messy locks, and took possession of my mouth.

I moaned. Hunger fueled again.

"I made plans for us today. You need to get showered and get ready. I thought we'd take a boat ride to Catalina Island. The views all around are absolutely beautiful, and there's this terrific restaurant I'd love to take you to." He gently brushed at my cheek with his knuckles.

"One surprise after another with you," I said as I sipped my coffee.

"You deserve it. I want you to feel the love I have for you every single day." He took a swig of his coffee from a large mug. "And I want you to know I love you during the day too. We can't always only operate during the night or we might as well start drinking blood."

* * * * *

Quinn

Motoring in a small boat on the Pacific Ocean, I sat mesmerized by the entire trip. I couldn't get over the scenery. Axel hadn't lied when he said the island was beautiful. Surrounded by clear waters as far as the eye could see, sitting by the sexiest man, I was in heaven.

With the gentle hum of the engine low enough not to interfere with our conversation, we reminisced about our childhoods. Several times along the way, Axel pointed at dolphins and even a whale surfacing from the depths of the water. Watching nature in its glory, I thought this truly was becoming the best date of my life. The sun's reflection off the water made everything sparkle, and I couldn't help but be enthralled by the beauty of it all. I'd lived in San Francisco practically my whole life and never once appreciated the ocean like

I did now. Experiencing it for the first time with Axel made it even more special.

Axel, leaning against the railing of the boat, wrapped his arms around my waist and pulled me into the shelter of his arms, lifting my chin to meet his gaze. "Watching your dark hair move in the wind is driving me insane. I've never seen such a beautiful woman in my life. You're stunning, Quinn." He placed a kiss on my forehead.

Axel turned me in his arms so that I faced the ocean, keeping me tight to his body. "Thank you for coming up here with me. It means more to me than you know." He placed kisses on the nape of my neck. He hesitated just a moment. "We're almost there. Are you getting hungry?" he whispered in my ear.

I stretched on my toes, turned my head to reach his mouth, and gave him a heat-searing kiss. "I am. Thank you so much for taking me here. It's nice to step away from the nightlife of LA."

He grabbed my hand, intertwined his fingers with mine, and led me into the restaurant, where we were seated almost immediately. It helped that Axel knew the manager and was able to get a reservation on such short notice. He had told me on the trip up how much he enjoyed this particular restaurant and how he would come up as often as he could, even though it took several hours to get there between LA traffic and the boat ride. The restaurant itself had a quaint, cozy vibe with an old wood deck that wrapped around the entire building, the view was even more spectacular here than on the boat ride up. The place sat atop a hill overlooking the ocean. The setting sun cast rays that danced on the water. All of it took my breath away. Throughout our dinner, I found it hard to pull my gaze from the view. I had never visited such a magical place before. So many firsts with Axel.

"So, what do you think? You've been awful quiet." Axel's voice pulled me out of my thoughts.

"There are no words. You have all these hidden jewels in your back pocket. How did you find this place?"

He smiled that sexy smile I loved so much as he reached across the table and gently stroked the back of my hand with his thumb. "Let's go take a walk out on the balcony. The weather's perfect. It's not raining for a change."

"I'd love to."

Axel waved for the waiter. He ordered two glasses of red wine, paid the bill, then gently assisted me out of my seat before handing me my glass. Amazed at how perfect everything felt with him, I placed my hand in his while we walked out to the deck. I inhaled the scent of the ocean as the heels of my shoes clapped against the aged wood. I absolutely loved the smell of salt water in the air. Facing out toward the water, I lifted my face to feel the gentle wind blow against my skin. Axel brushed up behind me, slipping an arm around my waist.

"I told you it was beautiful up here," he whispered as he nibbled where my ear met my neck.

"It really is. I can't even express how incredible this is."

"I'm glad you like it. I've never brought anyone else up here before, but I wanted you to share this place with me."

I turned in his arms, taking a sip of my wine. I tilted my head to look into his eyes. "Not anyone? I find that hard to believe with all the women you've been with. Surely at least one lucky woman got to be blessed with this special place."

"Just one," he whispered. "And she's wrapped tightly in my arms." He pulled back, taking my chin between his thumb and finger. "And, just for the record, I haven't been with as many women as you think."

I tried not to roll my eyes or laugh. I gently punched him in the chest. "I know who you are, Axel Rye. You don't need to lie to try to seduce me."

"What are you trying to say? Do I have a bad reputation?" he asked with a wicked gleam in his eye.

"The Great Axel Rye. Need I say more?"

"You know, those words could get you into some serious trouble if you aren't careful. You know what else *The Great Axel Rye* is known for?"

"Are you threatening me, you bad boy?" I giggled.

"I never threaten. I follow through on everything I say." He leaned down and gently placed a kiss on my lips.

"Can I ask you a question?"

Axel nodded. "Anything."

I was dying to know the answer. "If you grew up in such a bad home life, and your parents weren't your examples, and you never have had any other serious relationships, then how did you become so good at it? How did you learn to love? To show love in the way that you do?"

He paused for moment as if he were trying to remember. "When I was about fifteen years old, I lived next door to this surfer and his wife. This man was so cool in my eyes. He worked some sort of construction by day, but whenever he got the chance, he surfed. His wife was gorgeous, and probably my first real crush." Axel stopped and smiled. "I would look out my window at night and just watch them sit outside and talk. They always had a glass of wine or beer, and would sit under the stars and just laugh. They kissed, they cuddled, and they always appeared so happy. Their relationship seemed so perfect." Axel's smile melted away. "This was a huge contrast to my parents, who fought all the time if they were even together." Axel paused and kissed the top of my head. "Am I boring you?"

I shook my head eagerly. "No, not at all. I love hearing about your past."

Axel took a deep breath before continuing on. "Anyway, this couple next door was everything my parents weren't. It was nice to see... love. Well, one night I could see the neighbors in the kitchen fighting. I mean *really* fighting. My heart sank, because this perfect couple I loved spying on was just like everyone else. Just like my screwed up parents. And just as I was panicking that this perfect little world I spied on was about to crumble, I watched him reach out to her, kiss her on the forehead and whisper in her ear. He held her, and she held him back. He caressed her back as she clung to him, desperate for his love. No matter what, they had that. Love. I knew that I would someday have that. I wouldn't settle for half ass. I wouldn't settle until I was with someone I couldn't keep my hands off, and she couldn't keep hers off me. I wanted love that would be forever displayed. I guess I owe my old neighbors for all my mushiness."

"So you were a Peeping Tom growing up," I teased.

Axel started to laugh. "I guess you could say that."

We both laughed, enjoying this evening that belonged only to us. Nothing else seemed to matter at that point, and we were oblivious to all that surrounded us. Kissing, loving, growing together as a couple. This date captured my heart.

"Do you want to know how many women I've woken up to the next morning, Quinn? How many women I've taken to my own special places? How many women I have obsessed about, how many I find myself thinking of nothing else but them? How many women I've trusted my heart with without planning to? One. The answer is only one."

"Sometimes I feel like I need to wake from this amazing dream that I'm having. You're everything I ever wanted in a man, and why you've chosen me is confusing." I paused, searching for the right words. "You could have any woman you want. Someone who truly understands you and your life."

"*You* are the woman I want."

"Why?" I asked quickly.

"Why, what?"

"Why me? Of all the women you could have, out of all the women who want you, why me?" Taking a deep breath, he pulled me deeper into his arms. "Because you're the only woman who genuinely is interested in *me*. You seem to care about the man inside, and not just the exterior. I know it sounds ridiculous when I tell you how alone I've been, since I'm never physically alone, but lately I've been in a dark place. I have this vision of a traditional love. I want a connection and a bond with someone that can never be broken. I want to be able to look into my lover's eyes and no longer feel the shadows seeping in." Axel turned me so he stared directly into my eyes. "For the first time in my life, I feel normal. I feel a new reason to get up in the morning. It is you. You."

* * * * *

Quinn

I supported the phone between my shoulder and ear as I made some breakfast. I couldn't help but wake Harrison up early to tell him all that had happened. After coming home last night, I'd hardly slept. So many things overran my mind, leaving me lost in a fog. I had to talk to someone about it.

Axel had wanted me to stay the night, but I decided it was best to come home and wrap my head around everything that happened. We had not only had sex, but we both had admitted to falling in love. Axel still wanted to see me today, so he was picking me up in an hour. Being apart for long seemed almost impossible for us both.

I'd been on the phone with Harrison for a while now. He seemed to think my growing relationship with Axel was meant to be. Harrison was happy for me and happy that Axel had me in such high spirits. From everything I'd told Harrison so far about Axel, Harrison knew we were in love. Harrison even jokingly started referring to Axel as *hubby*. Then, unexpectedly, Harrison asked, "What does Axel think about the book you're working on? Did he give you a list of rules you can or cannot write about?"

I stopped and closed my eyes. I didn't want to lie, but I didn't want to confess my failure to reveal that secret.

"Well…" I paused to figure out how to make it less of a lie. "Axel and I haven't really talked about it too much." That much was true.

"Hmm," Harrison said. "Maybe it's better that way. He might be hesitant to fully open up to you. He may feel you are just using him."

I sighed with relief. As usual, Harrison and I saw things the same way. My reasoning on not clarifying things about my true profession to Axel held a little more rationale now. Although the feeling didn't last long as Harrison continued on.

"But maybe you do want to be honest. You don't want to start things off by keeping things from him.

But you don't need to talk about it all the time. Last thing you want is for him to think you're pumping him for information every time you two talk."

I hated the feeling of being deceitful. This shouldn't be so complicated. But if I were honest with myself, I knew keeping this secret for so long would upset Axel. Things were so good I just didn't want to rock the boat.

Just as I finished cooking breakfast, Felicity walked into the kitchen. She had a big smile on her face. "Is that Axel?" she mouthed.

I shook my head and mouthed back, "Harrison."

Felicity frowned and walked over to dish herself some eggs and bacon. She sat down facing me.

I cut my conversation with Harrison short, telling him I needed to finish eating breakfast and getting ready. I'd finished getting ready for a while now, but I could tell Felicity wanted to talk. I watched her shake her head disapprovingly as I hung up.

"You're going to lose Axel because of this stupid book of yours," she said. "Something tells me Axel doesn't know everything about what you're doing when you get back to San Francisco."

The lump that had formed in my throat during my conversation with Harrison seemed to grow even bigger. "I know. I'm just not sure how to get out of this hole I sort of dug for myself."

"Listen, I understand you aren't intending to bad-mouth or disparage him, but I don't think Axel will be so understanding. He's going to feel like you're using him and faking your relationship all to get close. It's going to look super shady."

I grimaced. "I'm not."

Felicity shook her head as she took a large bite of eggs. "You might know that, but Axel's going to see this book as a threat. How much does he know about you, anyway?"

I winced and looked down at my untouched breakfast. "He doesn't know I write at all. I haven't opened up about much."

Felicity's eyes popped wide open as she almost choked on her food.

"Please tell me you're joking." I shook my head. "You're going to screw up a good thing. I hope this lie is worth it."

"I'm going to fix it." I nibbled on my fingernail. "I'm just not sure how or when."

"The longer you wait, the worse this mess will be. You need to tell Axel." Felicity stopped and seemed to ponder what she had just said. "Unless I'm reading too much into you and him? You like him, right?"

I knew I was blushing. My face felt as if it had increased in heat by several degrees. "I do. I'm falling in love."

Felicity raised an eyebrow. "Love? Does Axel feel the same?"

"He says he does. Last night we… well we…"

"You guys had sex!" Felicity almost screamed. "Oh my god!"

I blushed even more and tried not to giggle. "Yes, and it was amazing."

Felicity squealed in delight after I told her the details of my first time. She clapped her hands together, smiling in delight. "I knew you would end up in his bed. Who would have thought that you would be the girlfriend of the infamous Axel Rye?"

"The whole idea really confuses me. I'm not sure I can deal with the drugs and the clubs forever."

"It won't be easy." Felicity grabbed the dishes and started to clean up. "Well, whatever you decide, I just want you to be happy. Be honest with yourself and follow your heart. Don't let other voices and opinions get in the way of what you decide."

Chapter 9

Fucking Vanilla With Sprinkles

Quinn

Axel and I headed to a new restaurant opening near downtown. I had started to accompany Axel on more and more paid appearances. The attention made me a little uncomfortable, but it was worth it if I could spend more time with him. Plus, being with Axel gave me a self-confidence I never had before. My introverted ways seemed to vanish when I was on Axel Rye's arm.

The place was crowded, and the media swarmed everywhere. I had taken a pill from Axel's stash about an hour earlier, and I was feeling a bit edgy. It was some type of upper, but now I wondered if I needed a downer to help counter it. Axel hadn't seemed too happy when I popped it in my mouth, but he hadn't said anything either. I knew deep down it was bad to need drugs to help me cope with all the attention, but I was getting in the habit of it. It just worked. Axel, on the other hand, seemed to be doing drugs less, and barely drank. He hadn't gone cold turkey or anything, but it did seem as if I was alone in using some nights.

As bodies swarmed around us, Axel held me tight while posing for pictures before he grabbed me by the hand, leading me past the people and into the restaurant.

"You don't need to walk the red carpet? Do any more interviews?" I asked, completely surprised. I had started getting used to standing to the side while Axel played the part of a famous person, but was really relieved I didn't have to do it tonight.

"I'm doing my part," he said. "I'm here and I've been photographed. I'm not really in the mood to do interviews." He leaned in to place a soft kiss against my lips. "I just want to have a good meal with the most stunning woman I've ever laid eyes on. Nothing's more important than you." God the man was good with words.

I couldn't help blushing. Axel always made my heart skip a beat. "I just don't want you to get in trouble for not doing your job. I don't want to get in the way."

Axel pulled out a chair for me after the host led us to our table. "You are never in the way. Never. You actually make this all a hell of a lot more bearable for me. I hate this shit. You know that. I just worry all the time you are going to find this shit as old as I do and stop coming. I also don't want you to think I'm ignoring you."

"I can't remember ever having someone make me feel so special before. I love how well you treat me."

He smiled at me softly. "Good, because *that* is what is important to me. I love you, Quinn. There's no question about that."

My heart pounded against my chest and my breath caught. I could barely whisper, "I love you, too."

Axel reached across the table and took hold of my hand. "Those are powerful words."

"Yes, they are."

He squeezed my hand. "I promise I'll do everything to make you actually *feel* those words every day."

I nodded and looked down at my hands. I took a deep breath. "Can I ask you something? Something has been bothering me lately."

He continued to hold my hand, softly caressing it with his thumb. "Of course. Always speak your mind."

"Why is Jillian always around you? Why is she always in the pictures with you?" Ugh. I was edgy from that damn pill, but it had been bothering me. Maybe now wasn't the best time to bring it up.

Axel exhaled, glancing away and then back at me. "I don't know, Quinn," he said. "I've hung out with her in the past, but she's always made more out of it then it really was. She's just part of the circle of friends."

I felt something inside me ignite. "Was she your girlfriend?" I tried so hard not to sound jealous. But I was. Even though I asked the question, I wasn't sure if I really wanted to know the answer.

"No," he answered softly. "She was never my girlfriend. I never saw her that way."

"Did you ever sleep with her?" The minute the words left my mouth, I regretted them. I hadn't intended to take the conversation this far, but the questions just kept coming.

I saw Axel's eyes widen for a second then go back to normal. He pulled my hand closer to him, gently. "Does it really matter?"

My stomach leaped to my throat. My head spiraled. What had I expected? Why had I let myself fall for Axel in the first place? Jillian was just one woman. How many other women would I have to deal with from the past *and* the future?

"So, she was never your girlfriend, you just slept with her? Is that what you're planning on doing with me?"

Axel's eyes narrowed and his expression hardened. "Quinn, I just got done telling you I love you. Would I say those words if I was planning on just sleeping with you like some groupie?"

I wouldn't listen. All I could think of was the fact that Axel had slept with Jillian, and it made me ill. "Was she a good fuck?" My voice dripped with contempt.

"Quinn, you need to stop." He pushed a glass of water my way and then reached for one of my hands again. "I think that pill is fucking with you a little. Just try to relax."

The lump in my throat had begun to suffocate me. The pill was fucking with me, but that wasn't the only reason I was upset. I did everything I could not to cry. I tried pulling my hand away, but Axel tightened his grip.

"So, are you still sleeping with her?" I swallowed hard. "Is it just part of your circle? No big deal?"

"Quinn." Axel's voice was calm. "There is nothing going on with Jillian. There is nothing going on with anyone. You are the only one I'm with and the only one I want to be with. Take a big breath and relax."

He moved his chair so he sat next to me. He wrapped his arm around my shoulder and tried giving me a kiss, but I turned my head away abruptly. "What do you want me to say?"

That made the fire inside me blaze even brighter. I knew I acted ridiculously. Jealousy made a fool of me. But for some reason, I couldn't fight back the emotion. I squirmed, trying to get away from Axel's embrace, but my struggle was futile. I was no match for Axel's strength and conviction.

I stopped and looked him square in the eye.

"I want the truth about you and Jillian."

"There was nothing between us," he insisted. "Even if there had been something, why would I lie?"

"Because maybe you still have feelings for her? Maybe deep down, you want an actual woman who is cool, famous, and who knows what the hell she's doing."

"What?" Axel's laughter irritated me. "No, sweetheart, the only feelings I have are for you. Only you. She's got absolutely nothing on you, famous or not. And she isn't really famous, her daddy is."

I stared at him, desperately wanting to believe the words spoken. But if I hurt this much now, only a few weeks into this relationship, how would I deal with anything worse? Being around Axel did something to my senses, my emotions, and to my heart. It scared me.

I shook my head, blinking back the tears. "I'm sorry. I don't know what got into me. Maybe it's the pill and I'm just fucked up." I took a deep breath. "But this is too much for me to take."

He glared at me. "What the hell does that mean?"

"I mean this is who you are. This is what your world has always been like. Who am I to think I can fit in to your life… your lifestyle? Things like this are going to keep happening, and I don't think I can handle it. You're famous and could have any woman you want. Women are begging to have even one night with you. I should've never agreed to—"

"Don't even say it." He took my hand and put it to his chest. I could feel Axel's heart beat against my palm. "You're scaring me. This sounds like you're about to end things between us. I can't believe you don't see how much I've fallen in love with you."

I shook my head. "It's too difficult, Axel. I thought I could do this… I wanted to do this, but I can't. Try to put yourself in my place. Would you be able to deal with other men constantly hitting on me? I'm so confused. I don't know what I was thinking coming into this. I let myself get caught up in all the infatuation and excitement."

Axel's grip tightened on my shoulder as he pulled my to face him. He stared at me hard, glaring as he spoke through his teeth, "What exactly are you saying?"

I looked down at my hands for a long moment, then finally looked back into Axel's stare. My eyes glistened, but I didn't cry.

"My feelings for you are what have me so terrified," I said. "If I didn't love you so much, I wouldn't be backing out now before it's too late."

Axel stared at me in disbelief. "Backing out?"

"I'm sorry," I whispered, casting my eyes back down to the ground. My head pounded and my body demanded a stiff drink.

"Stop, Quinn. I won't let you back out now, or ever. I can't. There's no turning back for me. You need to understand that I love you. I love you!"

He leaned over and kissed my forehead, then my cheeks and all around my mouth.

"Axel," I whispered.

He continued to kiss my mouth, deepening the kiss further.

"Axel." I pulled away. "I love you, too. But that is what scares me to death. I don't want my heart broken. You have the power to do so."

He moved a piece of hair behind my ear. "I won't abuse that power. You have to have some faith in that." He kissed me again, then held my face in his hands. "Trust that I will protect our love with everything I have."

A smile slowly lifted the corners of my lips. "You see how crazy you make me? Do you see how insane my jealousy just got? You really want a part of this insanity?" I giggled lightly.

Axel smiled, rubbing his palm up and down my back. "I understand it. I know what I do for a living and who I am can be a lot for anyone to take. I also understand that you being with me is going to be an adjustment. I understand."

I wrapped my arms around Axel and leaned my head against his chest. "I'm scared. I'm confused. But I do know one thing. I'm in love."

* * * * *

Quinn

Lying naked on Axel's chest, after another great sexual experience, I could hear his heart beat. I had never felt so content and so relaxed. I still had a lot of questions about what he wanted and what he expected out of me. Not to mention that this was my chance to really get some solid material for my story. I had been with the man nonstop, and yet there was still so much mystery there. Yet, in all truth, I was more of one. He didn't really know me or who I was. Writing was my passion, and he knew nothing of it.

I took a deep breath. I desperately wanted this to work, and knew I should come completely clean with him. Tell him why I came to LA, tell him why I took the job in the club—I should tell him everything. But what if he thought my feelings for him were a sham? He could jump to the conclusion that I was using him. *Was I using him?* Maybe at first… but not now. Things were different now. They were so different. I hadn't planned that I would actually fall in love with Axel Rye. That I would immerse myself truly into this lifestyle.

Axel must have sensed all the doubt because he kissed me gently on the head and pulled me closer before speaking. "I can tell you are in deep thought. Stop worrying. Trust that I would fight with every breath I have to keep us this way."

"I trust you more than anyone. I'm just still wondering about your lifestyle, or I guess, our lifestyle. I grew up in a completely different world."

"I don't think our worlds were that different." He laughed. "Never mind. Yes, they were." Axel soothed as he continued to stroke the full length of my back. "Tell me about your family. You never do."

"Not exciting is why. I was the typical middle American, middle income family. My parents never divorced, we had a dog and a cat, and we had family game nights. What you see on sitcoms was my family."

"Any siblings?"

"A sister." I let out a deep breath. "She died not that long ago. Car accident."

Axel tensed slightly. "I'm sorry. That must have been tough."

"It was. I'm okay. My parents aren't really." I shrugged. "Death is part of life. Hard. Really hard, but we have no choice but to move on, right?"

Axel continued stroking my back and placed small kisses on my head. "You are such a positive and strong person to think that way."

"She would want me to live life. She wouldn't want me to live my life in a dark hole. It would be a disgrace to her memory." I smiled and patted his chest. "She would have loved you."

"Ha! I doubt it. I'm not exactly the type of guy you take home to the family to show off. They warn little, sweet girls like you about boys like me, remember?"

"You are a catch! I'm sure there are plenty of fathers out there who would love for their daughters to hook up with a drug dealing, party boy," I teased with a giggle. I stopped my laugh mid-way and added, "But seriously, Axel, people don't know what they are missing with you. I honestly don't know why you haven't been tied down before. I'm never letting you go."

"It's really hard for me to truly trust people. For many women, being with me is just about partying and having a good time, and they aren't willing to give their whole hearts to me. Not that I wanted any more from them. Life was always about getting high and fucking."

I stroked Axel's stomach lightly. "I can't help but worry that I am too boring for you. Too vanilla."

"I like vanilla. Maybe with a dash of sprinkles."

I smiled against his chest, extremely embarrassed about my next question. "Are you ever kinky? I just assumed you were kinky." I paused for a moment before continuing on. "Actually, I don't even really know what *kinky* is. Forgive my virgin ignorance." I giggled out of discomfort. I was being such a nerd.

He chuckled. "I hate to break it to you, babe, but your virgin days are over. But I definitely can school you on some kinky."

Axel rubbed my head, lightly lifting my hair off of my back. He slowly moved his finger down my back until it rested softly on my anus. He applied a little pressure but didn't press in. My breath caught and I let out a soft sigh. He pressed his finger a little more. "How does this make you feel? Does it make you feel like a dirty girl?"

I couldn't answer. I didn't know how I felt.

Shit, this was kinky!

All I could do was let out a small gasp every time his finger pushed a little further.

"Quinn, answer me. How does my finger pressing here make you feel?" Axel softly demanded.

I shook my head and pressed my face against his chest. I couldn't answer. I didn't know how to voice the mixture of emotions. I felt embarrassed to have his finger invading such a forbidden area. Part of me wanted to escape his sensual probing, but another part of me wanted to scream for more. As his finger inched its way deeper, I experienced a slight pinch and burn that set my whole body on fire.

"Answer me," Axel commanded in a much firmer tone. He thrust his finger deeper, punishing my silence.

"Desire!" I whispered between my gasps.

"Good. How does it make you feel mentally?" Axel asked while pressing his finger the remainder of the way into my ass.

I shook my head again, hiding my blushing face against his chest. I didn't know how to voice the emotion. Kinky? Controlled? Mastered? Whatever it was, it was like nothing I had ever experienced. The presence of his finger had such a grasp of my internal struggles. My wall crumbled more with every second his finger possessed me. I wanted to just release and let go. Allow the feelings to rush through me. And yet something in me kept trying to fight them away.

"Quinn. Not answering me when I ask warrants discipline. Am I going to have to give you a spanking? Or maybe I should punish you like this." Axel began to pump his finger in and out. His action was not sensual or seductive like before, but replaced with firm and direct thrusts. The pace resembled an aggressive ass fucking, but it was still a seductive and an intimate act. I wanted to plead

Alta Hensley

for more, and at the same time, I wanted to beg for him to stop.

Axel pressed his finger to the hilt and used the force to push me even closer to his body. He pressed hard against my inner depths. My gasp turned to a moan.

"I know this might be hard. Hard to let go and allow yourself to enjoy such a taboo act. I want you to relax and allow the sensation," Axel coaxed. He kissed me lightly on the head as he slowly removed his finger, only to press it forward, past the tight ring, once more. "I'll ask again. Does this make you feel dirty?"

Without pause, I answered, "Yes. But I like it."

Yes, it did make me feel like a dirty, dirty girl. That was the only word that seemed to fit the rush of emotions coursing through me. I felt safe, protected, loved. I also felt seductive and nasty. But then the realization hit me. I felt sexy, womanly. And Axel was masculine and dominant. Everything felt so fucking hot, and so very right.

He slowly removed his finger, leaving me with a sense of emptiness. He then swatted me on the ass twice before pulling me closer into his strong embrace. With his arms wrapped tightly around me, I closed my eyes and relished the dynamic Axel had created.

"Are you all right, sweetheart? That was a pretty intense thing we just did," Axel asked as he squeezed me even tighter. "A small taste of some kinky for you." He chuckled lightly.

I nodded my head. "I had no idea… I didn't know." I pulled away enough so I could look into his eyes. "Why have I never tried that before? It made me want you even more."

Axel smiled before softly kissing my lips. "I like the way you think." Axel paused and took a moment to just look at me. "I need you to always trust that I have your and our best interests in mind. I will never abuse this."

"I trust you with my life, Axel. I'm scared, and I'm nervous. But I'm also excited for our future." I gave a sinful smile and added, "And I like kinky."

Chapter 10

Fucking Whack Job

Axel

By the next evening, everything returned to normal with Quinn. The drama from the night before seemed to have dissipated, but I knew the issue with Jillian would still be an ongoing problem unless I did something about it. So, when I saw Jillian standing by the bar where we all hung out that night, I figured it was as good a time as any to take care of this once and for all.

Jillian's eyes brightened, and she stood up anxiously when she saw me approach. "Hi, sexy." She smiled seductively at me, tossing her hair back. "I haven't seen you around without that little leech hanging on your arm all the time. It's refreshing to see you alone for a change."

I clenched my teeth, trying to ignore the comment. "We need to talk."

"Of course. We have so much to catch up on. I've missed you."

"I know what you're trying to do, Jillian. It needs to stop."

Her smile dissolved. "I don't know what you mean."

"Yes, you do," I snapped. "Stop acting like you and I have something."

She stared straight into my eyes. "What are you talking about?"

"You purposely try to pose in every picture with me. Or you try to stand by me like we're a couple at all the events." My jaw tightened. "I'm tired of it."

She shifted her weight and avoided my eyes. "Is this you talking? Or your needy little girlfriend?"

"It's getting old."

"You never complained before."

"Well, things are different now."

I could see the rage in her eyes. Knowing how much she loved attention, I worried she would make a scene just for some added publicity. I heard the venom in Jillian's words clearly. "You didn't answer me. Is this your girlfriend being a jealous bitch?"

I wasn't about to give her the pleasure. "To be honest, she's never mentioned you. Believe it or not, the world doesn't revolve around you, Jillian."

Jillian laughed, attempting to sound sarcastic, but failed. She slammed her drink on the bar, spilling the liquid all over. She glared at me, lip quivering. "You think I need you? If you haven't noticed, I'm doing just fine on my own." She lifted her arms and motioned at the bar around her. "I get invited to just as many of these gigs as you. And I have men begging for me to even give them the littlest time of day. And you aren't the only dealer in town you know."

"I'm happy for you. It's what you wanted to begin with. You've always been an attention whore."

"This is how you treat me, Axel? Have you forgotten everything we once shared?" Jillian screeched. She took a moment to regain her composure and smooth down her wild hair.

"That short-lived relationship is over," I replied, never releasing her from my glare.

Jillian returned the stare with her bloodshot eyes. She was clearly coming off a high from the night before. "You want the fame. You want the connections I have and you damn well know it."

"No, I'm fucking over that shit."

Jillian casually crossed her arms against her chest and gave an alluring grin. "So you say. You are a damn junkie, Axel. Not just for the drugs but for the fame. Deny it all you want." Jillian took a long pause as she scanned her eyes along the full length of my body. "You may be sexy as hell, but you are no better than a crack head begging for change on the street. You need me around."

My jaw locked, and I knew my expression grew fierce. "Jillian, you have a dark ass soul. You are so ugly on the inside that it's starting to seep out your pores. I want nothing to do with you. Please face that fact."

"Face what? The fact that you will never find this fantasy of a perfect woman? You're crazy to think that this no name suburban Barbie is the girl for you. We were good together, Axel. Power, control, ecstasy—our sexual need was always met… in all ways. Is this the life you want to leave for some unrealistic expectations? You want to run off and play house?" Jillian took a few steps closer toward me. "You can't possibly think that bartender is the woman of your dreams? Unless your dream is to end up bald, fat, and stuck with two kids in a three-bedroom house that threatens to swallow you whole. You don't want the misery of settling down and you know it."

I clenched my teeth, holding all my fury within. Her voice grated on my nerves.

Jillian smiled. "She's fascinated with your fame and your sexual reputation. The bad boy, drug dealing, son of a rock star." Jillian released a soft but evil laugh. "She just wants to use you like every other fucking female in your life."

"What I do from now on is none of your concern. I've asked you to back off and leave me alone. I will not ask again."

"Go to hell, Axel!" She began to storm off. After only a few steps, she stopped and turned around. "And don't flatter yourself. You don't have to worry about me speaking to you ever again."

"Thank you."

With that, Jillian spun around and walked away in a huff. All things considered, it had gone a lot better than I had hoped. I walked out of the bar feeling as if an enormous weight had been taken off my shoulders. I desperately hoped my problems with Jillian were over.

* * * * *

Axel

I looked forward to the photo shoot for a new, local social magazine. It was supposed to be a "What's Hot in LA" type of rag. I hadn't hung out with the guys alone in a while. I needed some good, quality bro time, and this gave us an opportunity to do so without the club lights and loud music. We took photos, laughed, and goofed around. Even though the shoot was technically work, we always made things fun.

I had just finished the last shot with Knox and Teddy when I saw Jillian rush toward me, looking very determined.

"Can I talk to you?" she asked.

"What happened to you never talking to me again?"

"Axel, this is serious."

I walked over to the makeup table to remove the pound of cosmetics on my face. "Go ahead."

"I mean alone." She glanced at Knox and Teddy. They both turned to me as I shrugged.

"We'll be over here." Knox pointed. They didn't go too far, choosing to sit at a table nearby.

"How dare you dismiss me just like that?" Jillian crossed her arms and stood in front of me, forcing me to stop. "As if I never meant anything to you."

I bit my tongue, not wanting any more drama, but I had Quinn to think about. "Jillian, I'm seeing someone now. I can't be dealing with you." I waved my hand up and down in front of me. "With all this craziness."

"She's lying to you. She is trying to do and say whatever you want, just to get close to you. I heard she got the job at *Wicked* just so she could stalk you."

I laughed, though I didn't find this conversation funny at all. "Trying to dig up dirt, I see. Don't you have better things to do with your time?"

"That's what everyone is saying. I'm surprised you haven't heard. She's never bartended before. But she used her connections to get into *Wicked* knowing you were a regular. This has been her sick plan all along. People are talking about it. How a nobody from nowhere somehow lands with Axel Rye."

"I don't pay attention to petty gossip." I did everything I could to control my temper. I didn't like hearing Quinn talked about.

"I don't mean to hurt you, Axel. I just thought you should know."

The inflated attempt to sound sympathetic infuriated me. The blood curdling in my veins made me want to scream.

I glared at her. "You could never hurt me, Jillian. I'd have to care about you for that. You know nothing about Quinn, so mind your own business."

Jillian shrugged. "She's using you. She's using you for your fame."

"Using me like you?" I asked.

"There was something special between us. I didn't use you."

"Bullshit!" I spat. "There was never an *us*, Jillian. And you know it. You made up all that crap to try to gain notoriety."

"I stood by you!" she screeched. "I was there every step of the way during your trial!"

"Yeah," he smirked, "signing autographs and posing for pictures the entire time. Not to mention feeding the press leaks about wherever I was."

"How dare you!"

The tears welled up in Jillian's eyes. I rolled my eyes and backed away. "Stop with the dramatics. Don't play the abused victim card. You manipulated me far too many times. I see through you now."

I turned and began to walk toward Knox and Teddy.

"You lusted after me, you asshole! We had sex, over and over again! We made love into the morning hours!" she yelled. "Don't you remember that?"

My stomach churned. I spun around and charged toward Jillian. I could see her eyes open wide in alarm, but Jillian stood her ground. I walked right up to her face and spoke through my teeth just loud enough for Jillian to hear, but my words were strong and cutting. "We never made love. We had sex: cold, meaningless sex. That's what happens when I get high and you take advantage of the situation. You knew what you were doing. We had one fucked up mistake! You used me, you took advantage of me, and then you tried to play games with me. You are a fucking whack job. I'm done, Jillian. Stay the hell away from me."

With her mouth half open, she stared at me. "I hope your vanilla girlfriend makes you happy. Because when I'm done talking shit about you, your career will be over. I'm going to say that you are manipulating her and forcing her to take drugs. I'll say you are actually abusing her. Sweet innocent girl turned to the dark side by Axel Rye. Now's she a junkie and it's all because of you. People won't want their names tied to you. I'm going to make you look like an abusive ass, and no one wants that around. I'll even say how you got me hooked, but I was too scared to say no to you because of how violent you got. How's the public going to take hearing that you beat women?"

"Blackmail won't work either, Jillian. But nice try."

"Fuck off!" Jillian turned and hurried away, face red with fury.

I took a deep breath and walked back slowly toward my friends, ignoring the whispers and staring faces of everyone who had just witnessed the scene. I was sure it would show up in the tabloids within the hour.

Teddy shook his head. "It's about time you told that bitch off."

I nodded, still feeling a little shaky. I hadn't intended to get in a fight. It wasn't my style, but I couldn't take another minute of her. I stood there, still reeling from what Jillian had threatened to do about Quinn. I didn't want my friends to notice that Jillian had gotten to me, but I couldn't even force a smile.

Knox seemed concerned. "Are you okay?"

I shook my head. "She said that Quinn is using me."

"Quinn? Is she?" Teddy asked. "She seems totally into you."

"You and her are a couple, right? Jillian's a lying bitch," Knox said.

"Quinn's lived a sheltered life before me. I think this whole fucked up fame thing is new to her," I explained, still feeling slightly beaten by the fight. "But I don't think she is with me because of the fame. I'm not even sure she really likes it." I sighed. "She never did drugs before me, though. I fucking feel bad as fuck for that."

Teddy shook his head, eyes closed. "Ah, Axel. You shouldn't have got her into that shit. You know how it turns out. Are you sure she isn't with you now because of the drugs? You know how powerful that need gets."

I shook my head. "No, it's not like that. It's different between us. Quinn and I have fallen in love. It's more than just drugs and partying."

Teddy paused before speaking. "I hope so. I like Quinn a lot, and she seems to make you happy. I just hope this doesn't end up destroying your heart."

"And screw Jillian! Who cares what bullshit she comes up with?" Knox added.

I eyed them both. My buddies had a way of always making me feel better. I could act as tough as I wanted, but deep down I needed their strength in my life. Feeling exhausted, the only thing I wanted right now was to be in Quinn's arms.

* * * * *

Quinn

An evening at Axel's home was exactly what I needed. I had fun at all the clubs and bars, but I really missed the peace and quiet. When Axel and I got to his place, he led me to the couch and threw his keys and phone down on the coffee table.

"I'm dying for a drink." He walked toward the kitchen. "Would you like a glass of wine?"

"Yes, that sounds really nice."

He walked to the kitchen and grabbed two glasses out of the cupboard. The open floor plan of the loft allowed me to watch his every move. I loved watching the way Axel carried himself. He had a level of domination mixed with casualness that made every action alluring.

"How was your photo shoot?" I asked, still watching him as he opened the bottle of red wine.

He shrugged. "The actual shoot was a lot of fun. I like doing things like that with Teddy and Knox." He smirked. "Maybe that makes me an arrogant ass."

"But? I get the feeling you had a rough day."

He poured the wine into the glasses and walked back to the living room with one in each hand. He handed the wine to me before saying, "Jillian showed up."

I stared at him. The words stung.

Axel sat down next to me and slouched back against the leather couch, placing both feet on the coffee table to relax. "I'd already talked to her last night when you were at work, telling her to back off and leave me alone. I called her out on the stupid games she's been playing. I thought that would be the end of it," he said. "But I should've known better. Jillian has to make a bigger deal out of everything."

I turned so I could search Axel's eyes to see if there was more to the story.

He took a sip of his wine slowly and then sighed. "She made a scene after the shoot."

"A scene?"

"A classic Jillian move. She loves the limelight." Axel hugged me tightly with a heavy sigh and pushed me back gently on the sofa. "Quinn, it's nothing. I wouldn't have even brought it up, but I didn't want you to hear about it from someone else."

"What did she say?"

He tried kissing me, but I pulled away. "Babe, let's not do this again. Seriously, the only thing that matters is that I straightened things out, and she won't be bothering you or me anymore."

"Are you sure?"

"Yes, she's taken up entirely too much of our energy as it is. I'm not going to let her antics get in the way of us. Jillian is out of our lives."

I stared at him for a moment, hoping he was right. "Okay."

Thankful the conversation hadn't turned into another dreaded discussion like the night before, I moved forward and buried my face into his neck. I pressed myself against the warmth of Axel's chest. I smiled and calmed a bit. Being this close to him made my heart do flips. I grabbed both glasses and placed them out of the way on the table. I moved forward so I was inches from his face and softly kissed him.

I gasped as his mouth crushed passionately against mine, taking control over the kiss. I clung to his shoulders, pulling him closer. Opening my mouth to the smooth feel of his tongue, I ached to feel his bare skin against my own. Sitting back, I slowly unbuttoned my shirt, my eyes never leaving his as I shrugged it off my shoulders and tossed it aside. His fingers easily undid the front clasp of my bra, parting it to stare at my breasts for a long moment that had my nipples going rock hard even before he pulled it off and threw it after my shirt.

A shudder rippled through me as Axel pulled his shirt off as well and then reached to gently caress my breast. He continued to ravish my mouth as his hands explored every part of my now exposed chest. I moaned as a hot surge of hunger rushed through me. I joined in by running my hands across his chest, softly moaning as my fingers stroked his nipples.

He pulled me closer than I thought possible. The heat between our bodies aflame, he groaned, "God, I want you. I need you." Placing hot, wet kisses along my collarbone, Axel whispered, "I've wanted you all day. I've needed you. I hate being without you for even a second."

I clung to him, panting for air. The heat of the moment, the fervor between us, was almost too much. My mind spun and my body pulsated.

"I'm taking you right here, right now. I can't fight this any longer. I want the taste of you against my tongue."

I looked into his blazing eyes and nodded. "Yes… yes. I don't want you to stop."

In an instant, I found myself lying beneath Axel on the soft leather of the couch, both of us completely nude. He kissed his way down my body inch by inch until his lips made contact with my yearning sex. I arched my back as he eased my legs further apart. Little by little, he began to place soft kisses along the inside of my thigh, gradually making his way to his ultimate target. I tensed as his tongue flicked the sensitive bud, causing me to moan in pleasure.

A wavering burst of intensity slid into my stomach. He continued to suck and lick, pleasuring to my very core as he used his fingers to part the folds of my sex, heightening my bliss, bringing me closer to complete ecstasy.

I tensed again. Wary of letting go completely, I tried to fight the wave of passion threatening to overcome my entire being. Having Axel in such an intimate position battled against my insecurities.

He continued to circle his tongue along the outer edges of my moist entrance. With a thrust of his finger deep within my heat, Axel whispered, "It's okay. Let go. You're safe with me. Trust me."

His soothing words, mixed with his sensual ministrations, brought me over the edge. Light

Alta Hensley

flashed, heat conquered, and hunger satisfied. I could do nothing but release a heavy gasp.

With greedy need and a mischievous smile, I managed to roll Axel onto his back so I could trace a hungry trail down his body. I kissed, I licked, I tasted my way down to the hardness waiting between his legs. I moved my way lower and lower until the tip of my tongue touched the tip of his cock.

With Axel's hips rising to meet my seduction, he moaned. "I want to feel your mouth wrapped around me."

I followed his command and took his cock past my lips, and gently sucked, swirling my tongue in small circles as I took in the scent of Axel's intoxicating desire. His groan, his shudder, and the way his hands grabbed at my hair only drove my need to please even higher. I worked my lips up the slickened skin, then drove them back down in a rhythmic motion. I pushed myself to meet Axel's demands. Licking lightly, I worked his body, intensifying his pleasure. Slowly up, then plunging back down, I worked until Axel's control snapped. His breath hitched and his moan reverberated through his entire body as he climaxed in my mouth.

The moment ebbed, satisfaction blanketing us both. He pulled me in close as I wrapped my arms around him and clung. I was his. I would always belong to Axel Rye.

A knock on the door had us both jumping up and scurrying for our clothes.

"Just a minute!" Axel called out.

I quickly buttoned my shirt and pulled on my pants. "Were you expecting someone?"

Axel pulled the last of his clothes on. He leaned over and placed a quick peck on my lips. "I'll get rid of them."

Axel opened the door to Teddy and Knox standing with beer and hot wings in hand.

"Are we interrupting something?" Knox chuckled.

They both walked past Axel in the doorway and went straight to the kitchen. "Did you forget about the game tonight?" Teddy asked.

"Ah, shit. I forgot." Axel turned to look at me apologetically.

I nodded and smiled. "It's fine," I mouthed to Axel.

"Hi, Quinn. You look… glowing right now. It's a good look for you." Knox laughed, continuing the tease.

I tried to fight back the blush threatening to conquer my face. I couldn't help but laugh. "Hi, guys."

Teddy grinned. "If we are interrupting something, we can leave."

I stood up and walked to the kitchen. "No worries." I opened the box of wings to see how many they had brought. "As long as you don't mind me crashing your party."

Knox had already grabbed the remote from the table and was flipping through the channels. "Help yourself." He looked back at Axel. "Come on, grab a beer and settle in. Tonight's going to be a good game."

Axel glanced at the TV and then at me. "Are you sure?" he whispered.

I winked at him and nodded. "It'll be fun."

Axel and I grabbed some wings and made our way back to the couch. We settled down, snuggling close. I had never really been into sports before, but I tried to follow along as best I could. Though Axel didn't make it easy, with all his continual kissing and groping.

I pulled away giggling from Axel's ear nibbling. "Axel, I'm trying to pay attention. You're distracting me," I said while I laughed.

"Cut it out. You two are like a Hallmark card over there," Teddy ribbed.

Before I could counter, my cell phone rang. I reached for my purse in a hurry. "Sorry, let me silence it."

"It's fine, sweetheart. Go ahead and answer it," Axel offered, placing a soft kiss on my cheek.

I waited to answer the phone as I walked toward Axel's bedroom so as not to disturb anyone. The men in the other room cheered loudly, and I started to cover my free ear to try to hear better, but by the time I got to the room, the call had already gone to voicemail. It was Harrison, reminding me that my first draft of the book was due. I had set a deadline for my own accountability and clearly was being anything but accountable.

When I walked back into the living room so quickly, Axel's eyebrow went up. "So quick? Who was that?" he asked casually.

"I missed the call. It was Harrison."

Axel smiled and patted the empty space on the couch next to him. "What's going on with him?"

I bit my lip, cringing, thankful that Axel focused on the game at the moment. I had promised myself that the next time Axel asked about Harrison I'd admit that he was my editor and I was writing a book, but now didn't quite seem like the right time. It shouldn't be a big deal, and yet for some ridiculous reason, I couldn't get the courage to confess.

I walked over and sat down next to Axel again, picking up my glass of wine. Careful to not further the already growing lie, I thought carefully about my wording. "Harrison was just saying hi. I'll call him later."

Axel's eyes narrowed a little. "I don't want to keep you from talking to him. I'm sure you really miss having him around."

"It's no big deal."

"Okay, I'm just making sure." He wrapped his arm around my shoulder and pulled me close. "I like having you all to myself, anyway."

I was getting nervous about not admitting what I did for a living... or wanted to do for the rest of my life. I should be able to share one of my greatest passions and dreams with the man I love, and yet I was keeping it a dirty little secret. Axel should know how much I wanted to be an author. I hated how this was turning into a huge lie right before my eyes.

I nodded my head in agreement and snuggled in closer.

Knox eyed us. "You guys really are sick. You know that?" he teased. "So who's Harrison?"

I took a long drink of my wine and looked at Teddy and Knox. They were both eyeing me. "My best friend, from home."

"You should have him come up for a visit," Teddy offered.

"We won't scare him away. Promise," Knox added with a soft chuckle. He got up and walked to the kitchen, grabbing another beer.

I sank in my seat. My nightmare of a lie was getting even worse. Now I was deceiving Knox and Teddy in addition to Axel.

"He's in San Francisco," Axel said, getting up for more wings.

Teddy clapped his hands. "San Francisco, baby! Let's go for a trip to see him! The club scene is hot there."

Axel laughed, sitting back down next to me. "Like you don't party enough here. You don't need San Francisco to corrupt you."

Teddy shrugged and took a swig of his beer. "Don't ever say I didn't try to help." He smiled and winked at me.

A fight broke out on the television that pulled everyone's attention back toward the game. I was grateful for the interruption and the distraction from the conversation, but I sat next to Axel feeling defeated.

Axel rubbed my back before asking, "What's wrong? Are you tired?"

I just shook my head and did everything I could to force a smile. I had allowed the whole Harrison thing to get completely out of control. I had misled everyone, and I couldn't sugarcoat what I was doing. I was holding back, and that was just the same as a lie. I could lose Axel over this. My deceit could end our relationship. I needed to come clean… but I was scared.

Chapter 11

Half-truths Are Still Fucking Lies

Quinn

After everyone left, an impulsive rush of courage hit me, and I suddenly wanted to come clean with the man I claimed to love and who also loved me. It was long overdue. "Axel?"

He looked up in response.

"I need to tell you something. And I really hope it doesn't change how you feel about me."

Axel sat in silence, raising one eyebrow.

"I haven't been completely honest with you about what I did for a living in San Francisco." I took a deep breath, suddenly wishing I hadn't started this conversation. "I write. I write for several different magazines, and I do some other freelance writing gigs. But my main dream is that I also hope to have a book soon."

Axel's expression turned skeptical. "Why haven't you told me this? Aren't you proud of being a writer? I'd think that would be something you would love to share."

"Harrison's my editor."

"I don't understand. Why wouldn't you tell me this? What's the big deal?"

I shrugged. "I don't know. I don't know why I felt the need to… lie."

Axel sat in silence, his eyes darkening. "You lied to me?"

My heart stopped. I couldn't bear the thought of losing him. I sat in place, paralyzed in fear. Axel's voice sounded so serious. God, was he going to break it off with me for lying? The devastation began to take over, and the tears that had threatened since I had decided to tell the truth fell freely.

Axel rushed over and put his arms around her. "Why are you crying?"

I tried to get the words out between sobs. "Please, Axel. I don't want what you and I have to end. I love you."

He pulled away to look at me in surprise. "Why would you think we would be over? I love you, Quinn Sullivan. You need to understand that breaking up is never going to be an option for us. I might get mad. You might get mad. But ending what we have is not going to happen. Are we clear?"

I nodded. "Yes. I shouldn't have hidden that part of me from you. I wanted to... I just didn't."

Axel embraced me and rubbed his hands on my back. "It's okay. We're still learning about each other. I don't like that you lied to me, but I wouldn't leave you for something so stupid." He gave me a warm smile. "I would love to hear about your writing. Maybe you'll let me read some of it."

I realized he had no idea of the entire story, and didn't assume I was working on a book that involved him. Looking at the man before me, I decided right then and there that I wouldn't tell him, because I no longer planned to use his name. Maybe I'd still write about the LA nightlife, but I wouldn't do it at Axel's expense.

* * * * *

Quinn

The next morning, I called Harrison early to inform him I wasn't going to do the book on Axel Rye. If I were to write one at all, it would not involve him in the slightest. His name was off the table. Hopefully, Harrison would understand and agree with my choice. I'd just got done leaving a message on his voicemail when Felicity walked into the kitchen.

"So, have you told Axel that you're working on a book yet about him?" She walked to the fridge, pulling out a container of juice. Her question was becoming her morning routine.

I looked down at my feet, and shook my head.

"You should tell him already, Quinn," she said. "Axel's fallen for you. If you guys are really as strong as you keep saying you are, I'm sure he'll understand."

"I know, I know," I said. "I admitted to him last night that I'm a writer, and I even told him that Harrison is my editor. But I stopped there. He has no idea that I came here to write a book that involved him."

Felicity poured two glasses of orange juice. "I don't know how many times I have to tell you, you need to come clean before it gets worse." She sat down across from me. "Do you plan on writing a book that paints Axel in a bad light?"

"No! I would never do that to him. There's nothing negative to say."

"Well, it doesn't look that way with how secretive you are being over something pretty stupid, which is why you need to stop with these games. Axel deserves better."

"I decided I'm leaving Axel's name out of any book I write... if I even write one at this point. So it's really a non issue now," I defended, feeling my irritation grow.

Felicity rolled her eyes. "So you think you don't have to tell Axel the rest of the truth. Come on, Quinn. Don't try to fool yourself."

I winced. She was right again. I knew that I owed Axel the entire truth. If the tables were turned, I wouldn't be okay with Axel withholding any information. I knew I needed to fess up. Half-truths were still fucking lies.

But how could I do that? I also still had a book to write. Could I still write it without using Axel's notoriety? Would it even sell without his name? Did I really have my heart in it at all? Harrison had already questioned me a few days ago if I really thought I could go back to San Francisco and leave Axel behind. I had assured him I could, and that was still the plan. But in my heart, I knew I would never be able to leave Axel. My life was spinning.

"I'm going to tell Axel the truth. There is nothing to be ashamed of, and I have no plans of upsetting him. This book could give Axel the voice that's been lacking in the media."

"If you truly believed that, then you would've already told him."

I saw the disapproval on Felicity's face. "I know all of this. It's that I'm scared. I don't want to upset him. Things are going so well."

Felicity got up and grabbed a box of cereal as she spoke. "It's time. I may not know everything about relationships, but I know that you keeping on this way will make you lose Axel."

* * * * *

Quinn

All day I got a strange vibe from Axel. Something just felt a bit off. My shame in keeping a secret had started to play with my mind, and the conversation I'd had with Felicity that morning didn't help. I kept wondering if maybe Axel knew about my secret and just didn't say anything. Maybe he was waiting to see how long it took for me to come clean. Maybe his crew had gotten wind of it. Especially since Harrison was already trying to shop the book, and it was about to blow up in my face. This lie made me sick to my stomach.

After we finished having a quiet lunch at a café and got in his car, Axel leaned over and kissed me passionately, instantly putting my mind at ease. This wasn't an act of a jealous or angry boyfriend.

"That was nice," I purred after the ravenous kiss. "I get the feeling that something is on your mind, though. You don't seem yourself today."

"I have a surprise." He smiled before leaning in and giving me another small peck on the cheek.

My mind raced, searching for clues in Axel's facial expression. Thankfully, it didn't appear as if he knew anything about my deception. So, from this point on, it could be anything and I would be happy.

"What? I love surprises!" I clapped my hands together like an excited little girl.

"You'll have to wait and see," he said. "I want to take you there."

I squinted my eyes and pushed out my lips in a pout. "Fine." I buckled my seatbelt. "But you're driving me crazy."

As soon as Axel parked the car in a large lot by a warehouse building, he turned the car off and leaned against his door to face me.

"Where are we?" I tried hiding my anxiousness.

"Okay, you know I get photographed a lot for my... profession... if you call it that."

I nodded. "Yeah?"

"There's a photo shoot inside that I have to do."

My eyes narrowed a bit. "And this is a surprise? Why didn't you just tell me that you had to work?"

"We *both* have to work."

I stared at him, clueless.

"The photo shoot is for both of us. The magazine wants a spread of us as a couple."

I sat motionless, stunned by the idea.

"I knew you'd be nervous. But trust me, okay?" Axel said while reaching for my hand.

My eyes widened. My face burned as if on fire. "No way! I can't do that. I'm not a model."

"I'm not a model, either." He leaned over to kiss me. "But you're beautiful, and I want you by my side. I'll be with you every step of the way." Axel grazed his lips across mine. Grabbing my face with his hand so I had no choice but to stare into his eyes, he added, "I want the whole world to know that you're mine."

"And if I say no?" I asked.

"I won't force you. I'll go inside and cancel."

"You can't just do it without me?"

Axel kissed me again, meeting my eyes. "No, because this was meant for me to do with you. But the choice is yours."

I stiffened and nibbled on my bottom lip. "Okay, I'll do it. But promise me that I won't look like an idiot."

"You'll be perfect."

My mind spun into overdrive. I had no idea how to pose for a picture. Did I smile, or look sexy, or try to pull off sultry? I tightened my jaw and stared out into nothing in front of me. My pulse beat so fast that I thought I might have a heart attack.

"What's wrong?" Axel asked.

"Will people recognize me after this?"

"Most likely. Is that going to be a problem?"

"Well... uh... yeah, I kind of think it is." I turned to stare at Axel. "I'm not sure I'm ready to be... well to be... openly dating..."

"A drug dealer?"

I shook my head. "It's not like that. It's just that you have a lot of notoriety and well..."

Axel looked crushed. "I guess I just thought that since you and I were..." Axel shook his head and reached to open the door. "Never mind, I'll go cancel the shoot. It was stupid—"

"Wait," I interrupted. "You're right. We are." I reached for Axel's hand. "I'd be honored to be by your side. Let's go do this."

Axel tensed up.

"What's wrong?"

He shook his head. "I'm not sure. I just get the feeling sometimes like you aren't telling me everything. Like you're holding back."

I stared at him for a moment. The door had opened. This was the time to just blurt it all out. Confess everything and hope to God that we could move on. This was the time… but the shoot. We had work to do.

"Quinn? Are you keeping our relationship a secret from someone? I didn't think about the fact that maybe you haven't told everyone in your life about me when I scheduled the shoot. I guess I just assumed that everyone knew."

My eyes narrowed, not understanding at first. "What?" I shook my head violently. "No, no! I'm not keeping you secret at all. I swear."

Axel didn't say anything.

"What's the matter?" I couldn't read the expression on his face.

"I just get the feeling sometimes that there's more."

The door was opened even wider. *Now. Now.*

I took a deep breath. A large enough breath to jump in the deep end. "Harrison," I said. "Well, it's not exactly what you think." I hesitated, nerves racking my body.

I watched Axel's expression change slightly. "I think I know what's going on."

"You do? I wondered if you did. I'm so sorry for keeping this from you."

"Why didn't you tell Harrison that we are together? Do you think he'd have a problem with that? Do you think he will think I'm a bad influence?"

The lump in my throat sunk to the depth of my stomach. I realized that Axel was completely off base. He had no idea the real truth about Harrison. I shook my head. "No, that's not it. Harrison knows all about you and me. Well, I haven't exactly gone into detail with him on how close we have become. But I'm pretty sure he can connect the dots." I smiled. "You are after all, Axel Rye. You aren't exactly known for your virginal ways."

Axel looked confused. "Then what? What's going on?"

Overwhelmed with guilt and fear, I sat motionless. Twisting my fingers together, I tried to drum up the courage to confess. I'd felt so many unfamiliar emotions since I'd met Axel, yet none compared to what I was feeling now. The fear of losing him made me realize just how important Axel was. If I were standing right now, the emotions would certainly bring me to my knees.

Axel kissed my temple softly. "Hey, whatever it is, can't be that bad. You're pale."

I looked down at my hands, picking at the loose skin around my cuticle. Every ounce of my courage dissipated by the second. There was no way I could let Axel out of my life now. The thought suffocated me, gripping my beating heart. I sat in the car feeling dazed.

"Quinn, what's going on? You're scaring me."

I attempted to give a reassuring smile. "It's no big deal. Silly really." I reached out and patted Axel's leg. "Let's go get this shoot over with, and then I'll tell you all about it."

Chapter 12

Fuck, Fuck, Fuck

Axel

Walking through the door of the photo shoot, I could feel the buzz of the room. The intensity of the energy almost seemed to knock me over with its power. This was a part of the whole celebrity craze that I really enjoyed. It was fun to get all dressed up and pose in cool and interesting positions, though I wouldn't be caught dead telling anyone that. That little bit of knowledge would kill my bad boy image in a heartbeat. The backdrops always blew me away, and I always loved the photographers—I enjoyed fucking with them which always livened the mood. I hoped that Quinn enjoyed it as well.

As usual, my heart raced at the sight of Quinn. I loved her natural beauty, but seeing her all glammed up was a surprising change. I bent down and kissed her in the makeup chair. It was supposed to be a reassuring hello kiss, but, unable to restrain myself, I kissed her passionately until the makeup artist cleared her throat.

Quinn pulled away immediately, playfully pushing me to the side. "You're going to mess up my lipstick."

"I can't help it." I smirked, pulling away with a sigh. "You've gone from the most beautiful woman I've ever seen to the sexiest woman I've ever seen."

"I hardly recognize myself."

I laughed, lacing my fingers into hers. "It's amazing what they can do, but with you they had it easy."

The shoot went really smoothly. It was easier than most, and definitely more fun. Quinn was a natural. Every time I glanced at her, I would catch a smile or a twinkle of an eye. It appeared that Quinn enjoyed it just as much as I did.

"Are you getting tired? Do you want me to ask for a break?"

Quinn shook her head. "No. This is a lot of fun."

I glanced at the clock on the wall. It had been several hours, and she didn't seem fatigued at all. With her focusing this much, the shoot was bound to be completed any minute.

I decided to make the shoot a little more intimate and brought Quinn's hand up to my lips and kissed it. I immediately forgot about the room full of people and the flashing cameras. I put my arms around her waist and pulled her close. "You're a real natural. I think you may have found your calling."

Quinn nodded in agreement. "I have. I've found my calling as your girlfriend. I'm enjoying this because I'm with you."

There were a lot more people than I expected in the studio when we finally wrapped up. Apparently, they had scheduled another shoot directly after ours. I knew the magazine was doing a full spread on the whole gang, so I wasn't surprised when I saw other people showing up.

I liked watching Quinn mingle with my friends. She seemed to blend in with the group effortlessly. They were becoming her friends, too. Selfishly, I hoped Quinn would create a whole new life here in LA and would decide to stay. The more friends she had, the better. This was a topic we hadn't discussed, mainly because I was scared of what the outcome would be. The thought of Quinn leaving killed me. But I wouldn't dwell on that right now and ruin a perfect day.

Teddy came up from behind, laughing, and put his arm around my shoulder. "So what the fuck? You replace us for some lovey-dovey shots?" he teased.

I shrugged. "What can I say? Do you blame me?"

Teddy playfully shoved him. "One word. Pussy whipped."

Quinn came up to us and wrapped her arms around me. "That's two words."

Knox walked up to the laughing group. "Holy hell, Quinn! You look amazing."

She blushed and snuggled closer to my side. "Thanks. It was fun, but I'm not sure if I'm cut out for all of this."

Even though everyone seemed to be in great spirits, I was ready to call it a day. I wanted to have some alone time with Quinn. "Well, our job is done. We're gonna get out of here."

"What?" There was a note of disappointment in Knox's tone. "Hang out for a while."

"Let's get some drinks and show Quinn how a real photo shoot should happen," Teddy added. He pulled out a bag of pills and passed it to Quinn.

I intercepted and shook my head as I pushed it away. I didn't want to be that boyfriend who controlled what she did, but her drug use—our drug use—was really starting to wear on me. I wanted us to slow down, if not stop all together. I still planned on having this talk with her, but was uncertain how to go about it. It was my fault she was doing drugs to begin with, so being the one to stop it seemed right, but at the same time it seemed damn hypocritical.

I pulled Quinn closer to me by the waist and she leaned her head against me. "It's been a long day. Quinn's tired."

Quinn's head shot up and she punched me playfully on the arm. "Hey, you can't put this on me. I'm not tired."

I smiled. "Fine. *I'm* tired."

Quinn laughed, and I couldn't help laugh with her. Her melodic giggle always melted my insides. Teddy was right. I was pussy whipped.

"Let me get our stuff and we can go," she said as she kissed my cheek. Turning toward the guys she added, "I better get Axel to bed… he's tired." With a giggle, Quinn walked off.

My perfect and jovial mood was soon cut short.

"Hi, Axel." The familiar voice I had grown to hate loomed behind me.

I was quiet for a second, hoping she would go away. "Jillian."

Jillian walked around so she faced me directly. "It's been a long time."

"What do you want?" I didn't want to be mean, but the last thing I wanted was any unnecessary drama with Quinn. Even talking to Jillian encouraged her enough.

"I'm not going to say I told you so, or try to make you feel worse, if that's what you're thinking. I just want you to know I'm here for you. I've always been here for you."

I sighed impatiently. I had no idea what she was talking about and didn't even feel like asking.

"Jillian, I'm not in the mood for your games. I'm done working right now, so I'm leaving."

"Axel, no matter what, we used to be friends. You're still a friend in my eyes. I don't know how

Quinn could do that to you, but I know you were really blinded by her. So if you need someone to talk to now, I'll always be someone you can count on."

She wasn't making any sense. The possibility of her being high or drunk was a likely scenario, so I had no desire to continue the conversation. "Whatever. I'm going to go find Quinn." I turned and walked away, leaving Jillian with Knox and Teddy.

No sooner had I started to walk away that I heard Knox call after me.

"Axel, can you come back here for a second?" Knox asked.

"I've got to go."

"No fucking way!" I heard Teddy confronting Jillian. "You're just trying to stir the shit."

"I'm not making this up. Go ahead and ask her. Ask Quinn for yourself," Jillian defended.

I walked back toward them, annoyed. "Ask Quinn what?"

"Jillian says that Quinn is shopping a tell-all book," Knox blurted out.

"Jillian, you have no idea what you're talking about. Get your facts straight before you start spreading rumors."

"Oh, so you're aware that she's writing a book? That she's here to get insider information? To sell you out?" Jillian asked with a smirk.

"Shut the fuck up, Jillian," Teddy shouted. "You're such a bitch."

"Fuck off, Teddy. I didn't do anything wrong. I'm not the slut who's using Axel for a big paycheck."

"What makes you say that?" I asked.

Knox piped in, "Just ignore her."

I was undaunted. "Well? Where did you get these facts?" I stood there smiling, arms crossed against my chest. A part of me enjoyed seeing how mad Jillian was getting.

Jillian shrugged. "Whatever. I was just trying to be nice. Believe me or not, but if I were you, I'd ask that little lying fake yourself."

"Just leave us alone," Teddy ordered.

Jillian nodded toward the direction of Quinn, who was walking back toward the group. "She's using you, Axel. Using you for all your connections and your name. She fucks you, whores herself out, and surprise, surprise, now she's on a cover of a magazine. I bet she'll use it for the cover of her new book. Maybe she'll call the book *I Fucked Axel Rye*. You're a fool if you thought this was about love."

I stood still, frozen by the biting words. I knew it couldn't be, but Jillian's words still hurt like hell. I took in what I'd just heard, then shook my head and viciously attacked. "There's only one whore in this room, Jillian."

"Let's just ask Quinn and end this shit right now," Teddy interrupted.

"Ask me what?" Quinn asked as she walked up and reached for my hand.

This whole conversation was absurd. There was no way Quinn could secretly be using me. I trusted her. I just hoped that Quinn didn't get upset by Jillian's accusations.

"Why don't you tell everyone how you're a deceiving, lying, filthy whore?" Jillian snapped.

"Shut your mouth!" I yelled, a red haze of anger nearly blinding me. I didn't like anyone talking to my girl like that.

"What? What the hell is going on?" Quinn looked confused and stunned by the nasty claim.

"Jillian, get your ass out of our faces before one of us removes you," Knox yelled.

Jillian took a couple of steps back. "Tell them all about the book. It seems your filthy, cock-licking mouth has been caught."

I lunged for Jillian only to have Knox step between us. "Get out of here, now!" My voice vibrated throughout the room. Fury coursed through my veins.

Jillian spun on her heels in a huff to leave and then suddenly stopped. She turned and spoke over her shoulder. "I find it ironic, Axel, that you are the all-famous playboy, bad boy, and yet you're taking it up the ass a lot lately. How's the ass fucking feel?" She smirked and quickly glided away, leaving her path of destruction behind her.

I turned toward Quinn and saw her startled eyes. I wanted to scoop her up in my arms and apologize for hours for having to witness that. Jillian was out of control.

"I'm so sorry, Quinn. I'll make sure that bitch never comes near us again." I wrapped my arms around Quinn and felt her body tense. She didn't return the embrace.

"Axel, I'm sorry, I should've told you this a long time ago."

My heart sank. *A long time ago?*

Quinn's beautiful smile and excited eyes had changed to a sullen expression. All I saw in them was fear... or was it guilt? It felt unreal, like some kind of nightmare. I searched her eyes for answers. Desperately searching for clarification. Reassurance that Jillian was full of shit. I searched for… hope. For a second, I thought I was going to be sick. My breath caught. This couldn't be happening.

"It's not what you're thinking," Quinn started. "I'm a writer, you know that. I did come here to work on a book. But I swear I'm not using you… not now."

My ears rang. I stood there, heart hammering. I took a few steps back. "You told me you're a writer. Tell me you aren't shopping a book on me." I stared at her, hoping I had heard wrong.

"On the LA nightlife," she said. "I meant to tell you from the very beginning, but we started to get close, and I didn't want to lose you, and I…"

Quinn's words echoed against the walls of my ears. Every word was like a punch to the gut. I wanted to vomit. All this time, Quinn had been using me like everyone else always did. I shook my head in disbelief and backed away even further.

"Axel, please." Unshed tears rimmed Quinn's eyes, but it didn't matter. I couldn't comfort the woman I loved. I couldn't reach out and dry the tears. I couldn't give... love.

Quinn stepped closer to me, attempting to reach for my hand. I recoiled, not wanting her to take another step. Teddy and Knox stood to the side, speechless. As the reality of it settled in, the shock and pain turned to anger.

"So, did you get all the information you needed?" My voice shook with every word. "Plenty of material gathered through your escapade with me?"

Quinn shook her head, tears coursing down her face. "Axel, please, you don't understand. Let me—"

"So, what the hell was I to you? I didn't think you were using me. I honestly thought you loved me."

"I do love you! I lied, but I swear to you that everything between us was genuine. I'm a writer, but I never intended to write something negative. Please, let me explain."

"I trusted you, Quinn. I gave you my whole heart. I had no idea you would do this to me."

I stormed away, fighting back tears, vomit, and fury. I needed to flee fast. I didn't want Quinn to see just how intensely she affected me. Those days were over.

Out of the corner of my eye, I saw Quinn rushing toward me. I didn't need to hear anymore. Whatever she had to say didn't matter. It was all lies. Everything was a lie.

"Axel," she said. "Hear me out, please."

"There's nothing to say, Quinn." I stopped and glared. "Unless you can tell me you didn't move here to write a book using my name. That you haven't actually been lying to me on a daily basis. Can you say that, Quinn?"

"It was my original intent. Yes. But that changed. I kept quiet at first about the fact because I knew you all wouldn't allow me in. Yes, I lied and I was stupid. But I was telling the truth when I told you that I loved you."

The words felt like a blow to my face. I spun around. "Don't ever say those words to me again. I trusted you! I don't trust many, but I thought I could with you!"

Quinn tried to grab my hand, but I quickly pulled it away. "But I do!"

I didn't want to ask, but I had to know. "Did you use me for fame or for money? Did you like all the glitz and glamor or were you just waiting for the big pay out with your book? Well, whatever. Bravo. Job well done."

Quinn looked as if she had just been slapped. "Please don't do this. Don't be mean."

Tears threatened to escape my eyes. Fuck! Fuck! Fuck! It was all I could do to not lose it and punch my fist through a wall. I had to leave before we made any more of a scene. I was humiliated enough.

"Good bye, Quinn." I nodded at my dumbfounded friends. "See you guys later."

I stormed out of the room without looking back.

"Axel, please, don't do this," I could hear Quinn cry.

Chapter 13

Don't Fucking Give Up

Quinn

"He's got this all wrong! I swear I haven't been faking my feelings just because of this stupid book." The tears streamed down my cheeks, no doubt dripping make-up all over my face. The only thing I cared about right now was fixing things with Axel. I pulled my phone out of my purse and started dialing Axel's number frantically.

"Give it a moment, Quinn," Knox said as he walked up and grabbed the phone.

I looked at him and started to sob, desperately trying to catch my breath. "But I have to. I've never seen Axel so mad."

Knox nodded. "I've never seen him like that, either. You broke his heart."

"That was fucked up, Quinn," Teddy said. "Axel really loved you."

I took a deep breath attempting to regain composure. "I love Axel. This was a stupid lie that I let get out of hand. I swear to you I wasn't using him. I've been nothing but honest about my feelings with him." I reached for my phone. "I need to let Axel know that."

"Were you ever planning on telling him? If it was no big deal, then why the hell keep the secret?" Teddy asked, disgusted.

Teddy walked away toward the photo set without waiting for an answer. I wanted to crumple in a ball and just cry. I had allowed this all to happen.

"If you want my advice, just leave Axel alone for a while." The disappointment in Knox's eyes stabbed at my heart. He turned without saying goodbye and walked toward Teddy.

I released another wave of tears, but quickly dried them up when I noticed Jillian staring with vindication all over her face. I wanted to walk over and knock it right off. That little bitch loved every second of this. The sad thing was that I looked a whole lot worse in people's eyes than Jillian did.

I turned and made my way outside so I could call a cab for a ride home. I broke down again as soon as I felt the cool air hit my face. Anger replaced my sadness. I was so angry at myself for letting such a stupid and insignificant thing get so out of control. This was ridiculous! I had lost Axel over something so stupid, and it was all my fault. All I had to do was tell the truth a long time ago.

Knox was probably right, I decided. Now was not the time to try to explain with Axel so upset. I'd wait until the morning to call him. I had nothing left in me to give anyway. I felt broken.

But fuck it. I had to at least leave a text:

Axel, please! You have to hear me out. I'm so sorry. Yes, I came to LA with the intent of using you. Yes, my plan was to write a book. But things changed. They changed. I love you so much. Please call me. Please.

* * * * *

Quinn

Glad to be home and away from the judging eyes, I reached for the glass of wine on the edge of the table and drank. I picked up the bottle of chardonnay and filled the empty glass, sloshing a bit on the floor.

I stared at the darkness in front of me, allowing the tears to flow down my face. I took a healthy swig of the liquor, steeling myself for the truth.

It was my fault. I lost Axel.

I leaned back in my chair. "Fuck," I muttered. I stared at my glass, berating myself for doing something so stupid.

Glancing at the clock, I noticed it was past midnight. Time for bed, if it was even possible to fall asleep. Cradling the half empty bottle of wine under my arm, I flipped off the kitchen light, picked up the empty glass, and stumbled upstairs to my bedroom.

Maybe one more text:

I love you. I know you don't feel that right now. But I do. I really, really do. Please forgive me.

I waited for a response.

Please answer me. Don't ignore me.

I waited.

Axel, please! You owe me at least a text. Tell me something. Tell me to fuck off. Anything!

I waited.

So, is this over? Really over? If I don't hear from you, I have no choice but to know it's over.

No response.

After climbing beneath the covers, I poured myself one last glass, hoping it would bring on the desired narcotic effect. The sun was already coming up, but I needed at least a little sleep if I was going to be able to face the day. Leaning back against the pillows, I took a sip of the cool liquid, letting it soothe my palate. I swallowed, welcoming the warmth spreading in my chest, craving the oblivion that would erase the pain of losing Axel.

Despair was the only thing left.

Sleep would not come. Who was I fooling?

I got out of bed and stumbled my way toward the kitchen. I needed to sober up and face reality. Trading booze for coffee was the only option.

The high-pitched, ear-shattering ring of my phone had me reaching for it frantically. I held my breath, hoping it was Axel returning the messages and texts I had been leaving. I reached over and looked at my phone. It was Harrison. I had left several frantic messages for him as well.

"Hello?" I stood at the kitchen sink, the cup of coffee in my hand, an ineffective antidote for my throbbing temples.

"What's going on? I couldn't make out anything in your message. All I heard was crying." Panic blanketed Harrison's voice.

Tears welled up in my eyes again. "I messed up, Harrison. I've lost Axel because I was a stupid fool." The tears turned to loud, gasping sobs.

"Calm down, take a deep breath," he soothed. "What happened?"

"I lied! I lied about this stupid book, and I kept it from him, and then it came to light in the worst way, and…" I blurted out the rest of the evening in a blabbering jumble of words, tears, sobs, and exhausted thoughts.

There was silence on the other end, then a sigh. "I'm sure once Axel calms down, you'll be able to explain," he said. "But it doesn't look good. That's for sure."

I wiped at my eyes and blew my nose. I hoped he was right. The thought of being without Axel killed me.

"It'll be okay. You need to calm down, get some rest, and give it a little time. I'm sure he will forgive you."

"No, he won't. He thinks I've been using him for this damn book! He thinks I did this all for fame!" My declaration, louder than I'd intended, caused an icicle of pain in my skull.

"Well, if you love him as much as I think you do, you'll just have to try your hardest to convince him of that."

I took a deep, consoling breath as I watched Felicity walk into the kitchen. Word of what happened had clearly made it to Felicity. I knew she had a lecture coming, or an "I told you so." I quickly ended my conversation with Harrison, promising I would keep him updated.

I sat down and tried to give a weak smile. Faking my happiness to my good friend would be futile, but at least I would try.

Felicity frowned. "You look like shit. I take it the rumors I heard are true?"

"Can we not talk about it?" I sighed as I sipped on my much-needed cup of coffee. "I already know what you are going to say. Yes, I know. I fucked up."

"Not an option," Felicity declared as she grabbed a mug. "Why didn't you tell him?"

I shrugged. "It's over. I don't see the point in discussing this any further. It is what it is."

"Bullshit." Felicity actually looked angry. "I see how much you love him. Your heart has been ripped out of your chest. Don't even try lying to me."

I grabbed a spoon and fiddled with it between my fingers. For the first time ever, Felicity made me uncomfortable.

"Seriously, Quinn. I don't understand why you have to be so damn stubborn. You love this guy. It's obvious that you do. So why are you so determined to try to destroy it? Fight for him!"

"It's more complicated than just love. He feels betrayed."

She nodded in agreement. "As he should. But you can fix this."

"You didn't see his face. It's over now." I took a drink before adding, "I'm not in the mood to hear a lecture. I'm letting you know that I'm leaving soon. I need to get back to San Francisco."

Felicity crossed her arms, leaned back in her chair, and glared in response.

I shifted in my seat. "You look mad. Come on, Felicity. Don't be mad at me."

Felicity continued to glare.

"You knew I wasn't planning on staying for long. I need to figure my life out and, well…"

The silent glare from Felicity continued.

"Stop staring at me like that! You're making me feel bad."

Felicity took a deep breath before speaking. "This is typical *Quinn*."

I could feel my temper rising. "And what do you mean by that?"

"You're a coward. You've always had everything so easy in your life. So the minute it gets tough, you are just going to run back to Mommy and Daddy. Go back to the easy life. Nice and boring and safe." Felicity had never sounded so blunt and harsh before.

My temper boiled over. "You have no idea what you're talking about! Not everyone can have *Happily Ever After*. Not everyone can have exciting. We all don't live in a fantasy world!"

"My life isn't always a fairytale. But I take chances in life. I take risks on love and life and hopefully will someday reap the rewards." She leaned forward on the table with a scowl on her face. "You're stronger than this. You have to stop living in your little, young, naïve world. You need to stand up and fight for what you want."

"Axel made his feelings clear. He won't even speak to me or return any of my texts—"

"Oh, stop that line of bull!" she interrupted.

I loved Felicity with my whole heart, but I had the sudden urge to rip her hair out. The truth of the matter was, I knew she had a point, but I still fucking hated it.

"Maybe you're right," I softly admitted.

Felicity looked up from her coffee with a satisfied smirk on her face.

I tried to swallow the ball forming in the back of my throat. "But it doesn't really matter now. I messed up, I managed to push Axel away, whether I like it or not."

"I'm not so sure about that. I think all you have to do is be honest with yourself and honest with him. I think you could work it out if you really wanted to."

I shook my head and fought back the building tears. "How? I lied. I chased him away when all he wanted to do was love me. He has no idea how much I love him and want to share my life with him."

Felicity reached across the table and grabbed my hand. "Then, tell him that. Swallow your pride and be honest. He's worth that."

I looked down at my lap in defeat. "I'm not sure that I can. I all but begged, and he completely rejected me. You should have seen his eyes. I fucked up big time, and I don't think there is a way to turn this around. I've called him so much, that I am two steps from stalker crazy."

"Well, I'm here for you. Even if you are stalker crazy." She gave a warm smile, which forced one out of me as well.

Felicity was a good friend, always had been. But sitting here with her made me suddenly realize how much I loved her. It was comforting to know I had someone to lean on. Many people didn't like Felicity Dexter, but I always saw the good. Right now, I saw even more. Wisdom. Felicity might be a tad spoiled, and definitely self-centered, but her larger-than-life attitude pulled you in. She exuded confidence and spontaneity. And she'd always treated me with nothing but kindness and loving support. Her reputation was no secret. She was known for sleeping around and being sexually adventurous, but I suspected there was more to it than I knew. Regardless of her past, present, or future, she was my friend and always would be.

She seemed to ponder my statement of defeat. "From the moment you met Axel, I saw the shadows in your eyes. Something has you scared, Quinn." She reached across the table and gripped my hand. "You need to let go of your doubts. You have to believe you are good enough. That he is actually in love with *you*," she urged. "You have a really good thing."

I swallowed and looked away. "You don't understand what it's like to be me. I doubt everything. Why would a man like that want to be with me? He could have anyone he wants, so why me? I'm not like you. You are so confident, so outgoing, and so sure of yourself. I have to fake my way through every social gathering. I live a fucking lie every single day, so it's only fitting I fucked up the love of my life by lying."

When I didn't say a word, Felicity gently squeezed my hand. "I want so bad what you and Axel have. I look on with envy. Not because he's the famous Axel Rye, but because I can see the love between you two. I know I put off the image that I'm some big slut," Felicity began, her voice breaking on that last word. "And I guess maybe I am. It's true—I do experiment a lot… with people. I just… I feel lonely, you know? Have you ever been surrounded by people, yet you feel so alone?"

"Yes," I whispered. Alone was not a foreign feeling for me.

"That's how I felt all my life," she confessed. Her eyes darkened to a stormy gray. "My mother ran out on us when I was six, my father was a drug addict, my older brother was overcome with rage and still is. And then I met Marshall in high school, and I thought life would be different." She gave a weak smile. "So I married him at eighteen. I had a husband, a man who claimed to love me, a man who said I was the most important thing in his life. But he lied. Marshall was always gone, off with his buddies and other women. He didn't spend any time with me. We were newlyweds, and all he wanted to do was *be with anyone else but me.*"

I sat in silence, stunned by the confession. I never knew Felicity had ever been married.

"I was bored. And lonely." She took a sip of her coffee. "And I cheated on him. Call me heartless if you want, but I was weak. I just wanted someone to love me and give me attention. I didn't want to be alone. I'd been alone my whole life. After a very short marriage, we divorced." She paused and took a deep breath. "I guess you could say I've been trying to find myself since. I'm just trying to find someone to love me… as broken as I may be."

I wanted to reach out and hug my friend, but remained still so she could continue.

Felicity picked up her coffee cup. "So that's it, my sordid tale. You think I'm confident, that I have no insecurities? That's a lie. I'm still the same timid little girl who cried and never got enough love. I'm a cheater, a liar, and I use people to fill my empty void. I'm not always proud of that, but it's my truth. And I'm lonely. Really, really, lonely."

Although I didn't agree with Felicity's decisions on how to deal with her loneliness, I couldn't feel anything but admiration and respect for the woman. And I couldn't judge her, any more than she judged me.

"You're lucky, Quinn. You don't have to be alone," she said softly, still clutching my hand. "Don't give up on Axel."

Chapter 14

Foolish Fucking Fantasy

Axel

I leaned my head back against the leather seat and closed my eyes, only half-listening to the booming music of the club. It had been a couple of weeks since I'd last seen Quinn. Still having to make a living, I had no choice but to make an appearance at the club where she worked. It wasn't like I had anything to worry about. I had moved past Quinn. I had no choice.

She had fucked me up bad.

Bad.

But I had no choice but to keep moving on. To do what I do.

I sat there alone. Not that I couldn't have found a willing partner to keep me company, but the idea held no appeal for me at all. After the heartbreak of Quinn, I was done with women for a while. Although the idea of meaningless sex to temporarily fill a void looked more tempting by the day. Nothing more, nothing less. I decided after Quinn crushed my heart that the whole "happily-ever-after" thing was just a foolish fantasy.

My stare moved to the crowded bar at the other end of the club. I didn't have to see Quinn to know she was there. Which was the reason I would avoid the bar at all costs. Plenty of people could stand between us, and I hoped I didn't have to see Quinn ever again. The pain would be too much. I shrugged off the dark thoughts and leaned my head against the seat again, thankful for the crowd of people to provide a shield between the two of us.

"Are you going to sulk all night?" Teddy asked as he sat next to me, handing me a beer.

I shrugged.

"Come on. You're going to have to face her eventually. Avoiding the situation isn't going to make it go away."

"It's over. No need to dwell on it," I replied as I took a large swig of the drink.

"So, you don't mind knowing that she's over there working. I saw her."

I shrugged.

"You're going to lose her, man," Teddy warned.

"I already did," I replied. I took a large gulp of the beer in front of him to try to numb the pain in my heart that Teddy was dredging up again. The past two weeks had been absolute hell.

"No, I mean if you don't get off your stubborn ass, she's going to take off and head back to San Francisco."

"She's leaving? What do you mean?"

"I mean, I heard she was leaving town unless you stop wallowing in your self-imposed misery and put an end to this breakup."

Panic sunk in at the thought of knowing Quinn would leave Los Angeles. "Have you forgotten that she used me? She doesn't want me. She doesn't love me. She wants what every other fucking person wants in this town. Fame or drugs." Saying the words stung.

"Ah, for Christ's sake, you have got to be kidding me! You know damn well that she loves you." Teddy placed cash for the tip on the table as new drinks arrived. "Let me tell you something about Quinn. She loves you, she's hurting, and she's scared. She's also unsure what to do and won't make the first move tonight. She knows you are here. But you all but slammed the door repeatedly in her face. Go up to her and make it right again. You are being a real asshole."

"It can't be right. It's fucked, and the only good that came out of this whole mess is she at least gets to be an author of a book… at my expense."

Teddy shook his head. "I don't agree. She messed up. No doubt about that. But she gave you everything. She committed to you and everything you are. I truly believe she'd give up the book idea if it meant keeping you. But let's face it, man. You aren't doing a real good job at fighting for her."

I looked down at my beer for a few moments before answering, "I guess you're right. I really fucked things up."

"You have to fight for what you want. You have to make her know that you will never just *let* her walk away. She needs to know you will always fight for the relationship." Teddy shrugged. "That's my advice at least, for what it's worth."

I nodded as I contemplated what Teddy told me.

"If you love her like you say you do, then you better get over there and convince her that you two are solid," Teddy added.

"I do love her. I wanted to spend the rest of my life with her."

"Wanted or want?" Teddy raised an eyebrow in question.

I smirked back. "Want. I definitely *want* to spend the rest of my life with her. But then, I'm not sure if I can ever trust her again. I'm still so fucking pissed!"

Teddy tilted his glass towards me and replied, "Well, I guess you better work through those feelings. She's worth it, dude."

I frowned, sitting up straighter, intently trying not to act bothered. I should have known that to think being in the same room with Quinn wouldn't bother me was dumb. Pain stabbed at my heart, and sucker punched me in the gut.

Switching my attention to the bar, my internal angst increased as I watched her frantically make drinks for the crowd. She seemed more frazzled than normal. No doubt she knew I was in the club.

Quinn turned around enough so I could see her, the ends of her perfectly shaped mouth curled upward, and I felt like a steam engine had slammed straight into my soul. My gaze trailed over her heart-shaped face, her satin-smooth and rich honey-colored skin, her doe-shaped eyes before settling back on her mouth. Lush, now only one corner curled up, lending her an innocent yet somehow slightly wicked look. It was the same mouth, the same look that had haunted my memories for the past few days. I missed her so much. No matter how hard I tried, I'd never be able to get her out of my mind.

* * * * *

Quinn

Axel was in the club.

I closed my eyes briefly, my heartbeat ricocheting a staccato beat against my chest. It felt more powerful than the bass of the speakers only a few feet away. Tears burned the back of my eyes as I tried not to stare at the one man, and the only person, I'd ever loved.

The same man who wanted nothing to do with me.

I tried to swallow down the instant swell of emotions as I finished my shift. I was done for the night. In the past, I would have walked over to Axel and spent the rest of the night with him. But things had changed.

"You don't have a shot with him anymore. So you might as well leave." I jumped at the venomous voice behind me. I turned around to see Jillian standing with her hands on her hips. She had rage in her eyes and looked like she planned to pounce. She was obviously high on something as well.

"I'm not in the mood, Jillian. Leave me alone."

"You're not welcome here. You intended on using Axel from the very beginning, didn't you? You're nothing but a lying slut," Jillian spat.

"This is none of your business." I took a deep breath to calm my temper. I tried to see the situation through Jillian's eyes. To Jillian, and everyone else, I was the villain. I had to remember that.

"Listen, I didn't mean to hurt Axel."

Jillian shoved her finger into my chest. "You are nobody. You don't deserve Axel, and you sure as hell don't deserve even the slightest bit of attention. I see your game."

Her comment stung. I no longer could contain my anger. I looked her straight in the eye. "No, Jillian, *you* are the whore. *You* will do anything, and I mean anything, for fame. You are nothing but a dirty, used-up woman who will never find happiness."

"You fucking bitch!" Jillian shrieked.

She charged at me and grabbed a chunk of my hair and rammed my head against the wall. I saw stars and my vision distorted, but I didn't feel any real pain. I was stunned by the attack. Who was this crazy?

She continued her assault by attempting to hit and punch my face. For the most part, I did a good job blocking her flailing hands. Everything happened so fast, and I was still stunned from having my head bashed against the wall; I wasn't really sure what happened around me. I realized I needed to fight back. It wasn't my style, but I had no choice.

I reached for the back of her hair and grabbed an entire fistful. I yanked her head back as far as it could go without snapping her neck. "Listen, you fucked up whack job," I yanked her hair even harder, "you stay away from me. You have been trying to fuck with me since the day I got with Axel. I'm over your fucking crazy!" I yanked Jillian's head, causing her to release a scream of shock mixed with pain. I hated that I had to be so violent, but did I really have another option? The girl was insane.

And the truth of the matter was I was fucked up. I was fucked up in so many ways that I didn't even recognize myself anymore. This wasn't the woman I was. I would have never been this… dark, mean, low, and fucked.

Jillian's scream caught everyone's attention nearby. All eyes nearby now cast in our direction. I glanced over to where Axel sat. I felt instantly grateful the loud club music concealed what was going on. Axel had no idea what was happening. I released Jillian's hair and returned her glare.

She reached for her head and tried to rub out the sting. "You don't know who you are messing with. I could have you fired for this. Hell, I could have you banned from every club in this town."

My rage exploded. "Do you think I fucking care? You have no power over me, because I don't give a fuck about much right now. Stay the hell away from me or else." I got right into Jillian's face, challenging her to push me past my very fragile limit.

I quickly glanced in the security guard's direction. He was approaching the crowd, getting ready to break up the fight. He surprised me when he gave me a small nod of approval, letting me know he was on my side and backing my decision to give Jillian a taste of her own venom.

Jillian leaned in and spat, "Fuck you! What are you going to do?"

The woman really was insane. Hell… I was insane.

I pulled my arm back, and, with as much force as I could muster, I brought my closed fist to the side of Jillian's face. The punch caused her to stumble back against the wall behind her.

I ignored the shooting pain working its way through my hand. "When you start something with me, you better damn sure be prepared to finish it."

I then grabbed her hair once again and rammed her head into the wall she was up against. "You stay away from me."

Jillian crumpled to the floor and looked up at me in disbelief. "Wait until I am done with you!" she screamed.

I took a deep, calming breath. I was out of control. "Do your best." I turned as fast as I could, not being able to take her any longer. I should have walked away before and hated myself for my actions. I was just as fucked as she was.

The fight was over, and even though I had lost control, I felt great. I was happy Axel didn't witness my temper because I was sure it didn't show me in the best light. But it was about time Jillian got taught a thing or two. And frankly, I had nothing left to lose. Who gives a fuck?

Getting ready to leave, my eyes locked with Axel's. For a long moment, we simply stared at one another, the days spent apart falling away as though they'd never happened.

Axel's face seemed to soften, giving me the courage to approach him. Maybe I was crazy, but I had to try. I had to talk and explain. I would apologize a thousand times if that's what it took. I missed and loved Axel more than I thought possible.

"Now's not the time, Quinn," Axel said, his voice barely heard over the music.

"Axel…" My voice trailed away. "Can we talk? Please."

His face hardened, losing its momentary softness. "There's nothing left to say. I've heard your apologies, your constant messages begging for forgiveness. I'm over it."

"I don't know what to do to make this right! I love you, and…"

Axel had already started shaking his head before I could finish speaking.

I wiped away the tears from my cheeks, but I saw the uncertainty in Axel's eyes before he looked away. I felt as though my entire world fell apart around me. I forced a smile shakily past the tears and nodded my head, finally accepting defeat. Axel was over me for good.

Exhaling a long, shaky breath, fighting back the emotions, I shot out, "I didn't realize our relationship was so delicate."

Tension in Axel's jaw and the glistening of tears in his eyes indicated that I'd hit a nerve. I had managed to chip away at the wall Axel created around his heart.

He stood up and advanced on me, not stopping until he stood so close I could smell the unique scent that seemed to belong to him alone. I closed my eyes, taking an involuntary deep breath, sparking the familiar desire that melted me and devastated me at the same time.

My gaze dipped to Axel's mouth—full, perfect, and inviting. What would he do if I kissed him? Would he push me away? Maybe it was worth the risk.

My eyes trailed lower, down the line of his throat, to the simple V-neck black tee he wore beneath his jacket. His chest beckoned to be touched.

"Don't you dare turn this around on me," he hissed only inches from my face. "I'm not the one who destroyed us. You are."

"Then let me fix us," I pleaded.

"Fix us?" he asked, laughing harshly. "There's no 'us' anymore. Our relationship isn't just delicate, it's scarred!"

I decided to take a huge risk and brought my hand up to Axel's face, trailing my fingers along the flush that stained his cheek, left behind from his anger. He jerked his head away angrily and his chin hitched up, but I saw the flare of emotion in his eyes before he jerked away from me.

My face inches from his, I ran my gaze over Axel, watching the wall crumble even further. I didn't want to stop. It was a temptation I couldn't resist. I kissed him.

The minute my mouth made contact with his, I released a low moan, my body reacting as though it had been an eternity since we last touched. I pressed closer against his body, forgetting we were in a busy nightclub.

Axel didn't just kiss me, he consumed me. His tongue stroked across the seam of my lips, demanding an entry I desperately wanted to give.

In a rushed movement, he grabbed me by the hand and led me out the doors into the parking lot. Without saying a word, Axel grasped my butt and lifted me up, placing me on the hood of a car, before pulling my thighs apart and settling within my spread legs.

When the velvet smoothness of his tongue stroked inside my mouth, I opened my mouth wider, meeting his tongue with my own in a hot, desperate dueling match.

"Axel..." I whispered against his mouth when he broke the kiss, running his tongue over my lips. I moaned as his hand tunneled beneath my skirt, cupping my moistened panties.

Axel's hand slid under the fabric and stroked over my mound, dipping past my silken folds. Pressing past my entrance, he thrust his finger in and out without breaking the next passionate kiss.

Feverish, I brought my hands to cup Axel's erection, my eyes fluttering closed as his finger pumped deeper within. I couldn't get close enough to him, couldn't get enough of his kiss, enough of his finger pulling the passion from my body.

God, I thought I had lost this. Lost the chance to make love to him ever again. My heart beat so fast I could barely catch my breath. I had Axel back. Axel was in my arms again.

I wrapped my legs around his lean waist, my body on fire from his touch. I attacked Axel's mouth with carnal ferocity, my tongue pushing past his lips to breach the cavern of his mouth.

I released a ragged moan, one that came from deep within my soul, from my broken fucked up heart. I had missed Axel so much, his touch, his kisses, but more importantly… his love.

With a low growl, he pushed away, turning his back to me, striding a short distance away, enough space to cool the heat between us.

"Axel?"

He kept his back to me, standing there in silence. Very slowly, he faced me. "At least it's clear what you've always wanted. I guess I was a fool to think you were more than just a groupie."

Axel's statement felt like ice thrown on the heat of passion that had threatened to consume me only moments ago. I eased myself off the hood of the car, heat covering my entire body as I met his cold, emotionless stare. Fighting back the flood of tears, I desperately searched his eyes for explanation. The sudden need to escape—flee from this pain—made my heart pound even harder against my chest.

"What are you talking about? Are you treating me like a groupie?" I could barely say the words.

What I saw in Axel's eyes now brought a pang to my heart. His anger reached out and nearly strangled my very being in its intensity. Anger for lying, for keeping my reason of moving here a secret, for not trusting in our love. Anger for destroying the relationship we had built in such a short time.

"If you act like a groupie, you get treated like one. An emotionless hookup," Axel stated quietly, his voice carefully matter-of-fact.

"Axel, please don't be cruel. It kills me—"

"I've been used more times than I can count. People I think love me, or even like me, for me, are just using me for a connection. I had no idea you were doing that. I was blind!" he snapped, his words like a knife, carving into me.

"It wasn't like that. You have to know that," I said, taking a step toward him before stopping, wiping at the streaming tears coursing down my face. "No matter what you now believe, I… I love you."

"Love me?" He laughed with venom. "You fucked with me," he said, anger tightening his features. "You wanted the inside scoop on Axel Rye, son of the all mighty Jamison Rye. You lived the party scene and snorted my coke up your nose. And you fucked with me! Nothing different than all the other groupies of my life." Fire burned in his eyes.

Unable to stand seeing the pain in Axel's eyes, I turned. My voice low, I said, "I was insecure. I was afraid that any wrong step I made would mean losing you. I didn't have enough faith in us as a couple. I guess I didn't have enough trust in you. I should have told you the truth. It was the stupidest thing I could have done." I stopped, taking a deep breath as a sob choked me. "I—I was acting like a stupid love-struck child. I created drama that didn't need to exist."

I stopped, my throat clogged with grief, blinking rapidly in an attempt to stop the tears burning my eyes. Afraid if I kept crying, I'd never be able to stop. I fought to keep it together, forcing myself to go on.

"I'm sorry, Axel. I owed you the truth about what I do for a living and this stupid book. I just didn't know what to do as the lie grew each time I let you believe otherwise," I said, offering a helpless shake of my head. "I made it a bigger deal than it was." I paused and drew in a breath. "And it was probably the biggest mistake I've ever made. I didn't mean to hurt you." I paused before continuing. "I wasn't using you. I wasn't faking my desire to be with you. I wanted what you wanted, but I don't expect you to believe me. I know I lost that trust. I'm so sorry." I merely whispered my last words.

As if a miracle just happened, Axel strode over to me, dragging me into his arms, holding me close. "Quinn, didn't you know how *much* I loved you?" he asked, pulling away enough to stare into my face. "That if you had just told me the truth, I would have understood? I wouldn't have acted like an asshole. I would have trusted in our love. You were my world," he said as he brushed his fingertips over my tear-stained cheeks, cupping my face with his palms.

"Then forgive me," I whispered.

"I loved you. I pictured building a life with you. When you got caught in the lie, my entire world crumbled. All those dreams I had, they were dreams of us, places I wanted to go... with you." Axel glared. "I wanted to be with you. Didn't you know that?"

I saw tenderness and hurt mingled in his eyes. I also saw lingering anger, an anger I deserved.

"I'm sorry." That was all I could verbalize right then. So many conflicting emotions coursed throughout my body that I felt almost crushed by the weight of them as I moved my hand slowly to Axel's. Tears pooled in my eyes, burning them. But I willed myself to hold them back for once.

"I know you are," he finally whispered.

"I'll do whatever it takes to make this right with you," I said, seeming to find my voice. "I want to earn back your trust. Do you want me to stop writing the book? I wasn't going to use your name, but I will stop writing it altogether if you want." Even though I made the offer, deep down I didn't know if I would be able to follow through with that. I didn't know how far Harrison had gone with it.

Axel shook his head, his voice even as he spoke. "I don't expect you to do that. I would never ask that of you." He sighed and ran a hand through his hair, his eyes moving heavenward for a moment. "I guess I've known that you never really used me. Your intent at the beginning maybe was to, but I have to have faith in knowing you didn't mean to hurt me—at least not once we fell in love. It was just a lie, but I know, deep down, that your heart has been in the right place."

"I know that none of this would have happened if I had just trusted that you would understand," I murmured. "This shouldn't have been an issue." The tears I had held back finally gave way. "I embarrassed you in front of your friends."

Axel shook his head. "You don't need to worry about them. They've seen a lot more drama than that."

"I don't want them to ever doubt my love for you. I don't want *you* to ever doubt my love, either."

"That's a tough one," he murmured in a voice so quiet I almost didn't hear him. But I did, and the tears fell faster.

"You cared about me once," I said as I wiped at my moist face. "Maybe you could learn to care about me again—someday?" I sounded like a little girl desperate for affection and I hated it, but I needed Axel. I wanted Axel. Not just because he made me feel appreciated and cared for, but because when I was in his arms, I felt complete. And I loved Axel and hoped our love deserved another chance.

"I didn't stop caring about you. I'll always care about you and want what's best for you."

"*You* are what is best for me."

Axel shook his head. "I wish I could say I one hundred percent believed that. Because you stole my heart the day I saw you in the club." He smiled a bit. "But that was... like a dream, Quinn. We lived this fast and furious love affair that maybe was always bound to come crashing down."

"Don't say that," I pleaded. "Don't give up on us. Please."

"I think I'm just facing reality."

"Do you love me enough to stay with me?" I asked as more tears slid down my face.

"I love you. I have since I met you. The whole issue with this book and Harrison reminded me that you still have a life in San Francisco. You still plan on going back and building your career. As much as I want to be selfish and just take you in my arms, make love to you and promise you everything will be all right, I can't. I know that long-distance relationships don't work out."

"I decided long ago, long before this whole mess, that I was staying here... with you," I cried.

Axel looked moved by my admission and slowly pulled me close to his chest. I closed my eyes for a brief moment as I felt a whisper of a touch on my face as he began to dab at my tears with the pads of his warm, gentle fingertips.

"I think you need to move back," he said in a hushed voice as I opened my eyes and stared at him in shock. "I can't do this."

In one swift motion, Axel turned around and walked back in the club without saying another word, leaving me standing there stunned.

What the fuck just happened?

We were so close.

So close.

And just as I was about to crumble to my knees and give up on everything, a sound from the depths of hell occurred.

Chapter 15

Fucking Jillian

Quinn

"You don't know who you fucking messed with!" I jumped at the wicked declaration suddenly right behind me. I turned around to see Jillian standing with a knife pointed in my direction. Her dilated eyes revealed an evil inside. Drugs, alcohol, hatred, and a weapon made a deadly mix. My heart stopped as Jillian charged.

My head whipped back from the force of the blow. Blood shot from the corner of my mouth as Jillian's knuckles made contact with my lower lip. The evil in her eyes shone in the dim light of the parking lot. The stench of her breath only added to the demon-like figure before me.

Swiping my fingertips over my mouth, I struggled to my feet, but Jillian was suddenly on top of me, her fishnet-clad thighs straddling my chest, pinning me to the cold asphalt below. I tried not to focus on the crazed face looming over me. Her face showed a fury that made me realize she would indeed try to kill me. She was too far gone to stop in her attack.

I had knocked the knife out of Jillian's hand when she unexpectedly lunged at me. But the knife remained within my reach. If only I could stretch out my arm and—

"Stop fighting me, bitch! I'm going to show you what happens when you mess with me. Do you know who I am? How dare you punch me in the club! You'll pay for that now!"

I blocked the pummel of hands, feeling Jillian's skin beneath my nails as I clawed at her face. I let out a scream even though no one would hear. The music in the club was too loud. No one was there to save me. I had no choice but to save myself.

Jillian grunted, beads of sweat dripping off her forehead. I could feel Jillian's strength weakening. Hope washed over me. I could still fight her off. I just needed to outlast her power. Stamina and sobriety could save my life.

Jillian was breathing hard, her scrawny body heaving from each jagged pant. She had me trapped on the cold ground, but I knew I had a chance to break free as Jillian's energy faded. I struggled to draw air into my lungs, but Jillian's weight on my stomach almost suffocated me. I couldn't wrestle out from her hold, let alone take a breath. My own energy faded just as fast. I sucked in much-needed oxygen, refusing to look at Jillian's disgusting face only inches from my own as she continued to punch at my head. From the corner of my eye, I saw a flash of silver.

Her knife. I needed to reach her knife.

Reach for the knife.

I forced myself to be brave. I took a calming breath to steady my nerves. I breathed evenly through my nose, slowly counting to five. I could do this. I had to do this. I had to fight back, or Jillian would kill me.

Before Jillian could react, my hand reached out, fingers connecting with the silver handle of the knife. When Jillian realized what I was doing, she lunged for the blade. But she wasn't fast enough. Her eyes bulged in shock just as I stuck the blade into her upper arm.

Jillian screamed as she glanced down at her bloody arm in horror. Her dark eyes flashed with rage as she knocked the knife out of my hand, sending it flying across the ground. Jillian grabbed a hold of my neck and squeezed with a renewed, superhuman strength. Struggling for air, I realized I was going to die by Jillian's hand. I had missed my chance.

* * * * *

Axel

My chest felt heavy as I walked back into the club. The realization that Quinn had probably left by now made my throat tighten, but knowing I was the one who'd turned my back on her hurt even more.

Go to her.

Those three words repeated over and over again in my mind, screamed from my soul.

I walked halfway to the VIP area when I finally couldn't stand it anymore. I had to see if Quinn was still out there. Maybe she hadn't left yet. Maybe I still had the chance to make things right. I *needed* to make it right.

I threw open the back door and froze in place, panic rising in my body as I watched the scene before me. With a burst of rage, I charged toward Quinn. She lay flat on her back, with Jillian on top of her, choking the life right out of her.

Suddenly Quinn snapped into a state of alertness, landing a nasty punch to Jillian's jaw. Quinn reached to grab a jagged rock near her hand, crashing it down on the side of Jillian's head. The blow sent her into unconsciousness and she collapsed on top of Quinn.

The silence deafening, I surged toward Quinn. "God, Quinn! Are you okay?" I pulled her from under Jillian's body.

* * * * *

Quinn

The sound of Axel's voice brought tears to my eyes. He was here! Help... a miracle... Axel was here.

Almost instantly, my entire body began to shake. My breath came out in ragged gasps. Air. I needed air. Jillian was dead! I killed someone! I took another's life!

"I'm here, Quinn. Everything's going to be okay." I felt Axel's hand on my forearm. Blinking with confusion, I looked down and saw that my bloody hand still gripped the rock.

"I killed her! Oh my god!"

Axel placed his hand on Jillian's throat and checked for a pulse. "No. She's alive." He pulled his cell phone out of his pocket and dialed 911. In a hurry, he explained the situation to dispatch and demanded they send the police and ambulance.

"It's okay, Quinn. You were defending yourself." The soft reassurance of his voice soothed me. I loosened my grip on the rock and let it fall to the ground.

"Are you all right?" he asked gruffly.

I stared into his dark eyes for a long moment before finally whispering, "No." And then I threw myself at him, needing his strength.

I clung to him desperately as I sobbed for what felt like a lifetime. Weak from exhaustion, my body collapsed against his. The next thing I knew, I was in his arms, and he stroked my back with his big, warm hands. "It's all right," he said softly. "You're all right now."

He pulled back slightly, remorse clouding his shadowed eyes. "I'm so sorry. I should have never left you."

Tears stung my eyes. "I'm sorry I put you in a situation that you felt you had to. I know you may never trust me again."

Axel's features creased with remorse. "I left you, and you got attacked. It's all my fault."

"You had no way of knowing."

Axel looked ready to argue, but a shout from behind put an end to the conversation. I turned to see two police officers immediately hurry toward Jillian's unconscious form.

"What happened?" the cop demanded, his steely eyes fixed on me and Axel.

In a calm yet firm voice, Axel told the officers everything. When he finished, he glanced at me and smiled. It was a smile that let me know it truly would be all right. Everything would be fine... with Axel.

After hours of answering questions and filling out paperwork, we were finally free to go. I felt relief when Jillian regained consciousness as the paramedics arrived. No matter what, I didn't want to hurt her, and definitely didn't want to kill her. The incident was the most terrifying experience of my life. I refused to press charges even though the police urged me to do so. At the end of the day, Jillian needed help. Not jail, but help with her demons, and definitely help with her addictions.

Axel escorted me to the limo and gently assisted me inside. "Do you hurt? You have cuts and bruises."

"A little, but I'll be fine."

Axel watched me intently. His eyes shone with so much protectiveness. So much uncertainty. He reached out, cupping the right side of my face ever so gently in the palm of his hand. "We're going to the hospital to get everything checked out."

"I'm fine. Please, I don't want to go to the hospital. I have some cuts and bruises. That's all. The paramedics already checked me out. Please."

Axel sighed. "Fine, but you're staying with me tonight. Don't even try arguing. I'm not asking, I'm telling."

I blinked back more tears and he leaned forward and slowly, reverently, pressed a kiss to my bruised cheek. He repeated the gesture, kissing my cut cheekbone, then the bridge of my bloody nose, the curve of my beaten jaw, my eyelid. Finally, he found my mouth and pressed his lips to mine. I started to cry as he pulled me close and wrapped his arms around me.

"I'm not going anywhere, Quinn. I will never leave your side again."

"Oh, god," I said, my hands curling into the fabric of his shirt as I pulled him closer, almost as though I tried to merge my body with his. "You have no idea how afraid I was."

Axel nodded. "I'll never let Jillian near you again."

I shook my head. "No. I don't care about Jillian and that whole incident. It's over. I was so scared of losing… you."

"Never again," he whispered as he dropped a kiss onto my forehead.

I leaned into him deeper. "You'll forgive me?" I asked and rested my tear-stained face in the crook of Axel's neck for a moment. His hand found my back and massaged it lightly in small circles for a long moment.

"I can't stand seeing you cry." He leaned over and kissed my damp cheek. "I love you."

"Let's go to your place and work things out. Let us start over, please. Let's make us whole again," I pleaded. "Forgive me and love me again."

Chapter 16

No More Fucks

Axel

With uncertainty and nerves twisting my stomach, the night was an emotional blur. The entire ride to my place, was filled with relief to have Quinn sitting safely beside me, mixed with confusion and pain I couldn't quite shake off. I didn't know what to expect when we got home. My mind working in overdrive, I closed my eyes to try to clear my thoughts.

Quinn reached for my hand, and the soft touch made my heart leap out of my chest. I didn't want to face the woman I so desperately loved only to see betrayal. I couldn't give her reassurance, so I gently pulled my hand free. Silence was the only thing I could offer.

"Axel? I'd really like to show you something if I can."

I didn't want to be dramatic and continue with my fury, call off the relationship, or do any other rash action that ran through my head. At the end of the day, I loved her completely. Seeing her hurt only intensified my feelings for her. She was everything I could ever dream of. I wanted to make this work. Quinn had already surrendered her love and given her entire heart. It was obvious. And she was sorry. That much was obvious. But could I trust her?

She reached into her purse and pulled out a bunch of papers wrapped in a rubber band.

"What is all that?"

"I've been keeping these in my bag ever since… well ever since in hopes to show you why I do what I do. They're all of the magazine and newspaper articles, and small essays I've ever written." She pointed to her name on one of them, and then pointed to her name on another. "See that?"

I read her written name, confused. "Your name?"

"Yes, my name. Quinn Sullivan."

"I don't understand."

"When I was a child, my grandmother always told me that I had a name that should be lit up in lights. I had a name worthy of a queen. She told me that with a name like Quinn Sullivan, I was destined for success." She paused to take a deep breath. "Every time I place my name on something I write, I feel like I am honoring my grandmother's memory." She took another deep breath and continued on. "There was not a lot of love in my home growing up. My parents weren't affectionate and rarely offered praise. It wasn't a bad childhood or anything. Just cold. But things were different with my grandmother. She made me feel like the most special person in the world. Her words and encouragement made me feel like I could do whatever I wanted. She actually made me believe I was destined for great things." She paused as she wiped at a falling tear. "She made me promise to do something special with my life. She made me promise to make Quinn Sullivan a name not to be forgotten. She made me promise to shoot for my dreams, because with a name like mine, dreams would come to reality. It doesn't excuse my lies…"

I reached for Quinn's hand and linked my fingers through hers. I offered a smile, finding it impossible to be angry at the woman before me. She squeezed her fingers tightly between mine, and a shiver of satisfaction went through me. The simplest touch confirmed that Quinn was the only woman I would ever need.

Quinn was here… fighting. Confiding in me like she'd never done before. Deep down I'd hoped she would come to me, that the bond between us was as powerful as I believed. It had been weeks and I had tried my best to forget all about her, blocking the painful memories of her lies from my mind.

But here she was, sitting before me with her face shadowed in the dim light of the passing streetlights. She was a woman of such beauty that she took my breath away. Her skin was smooth, golden—gorgeous even with the bruises and cuts. Her hair an enchanting brown, richer and deeper than any woman's I'd seen. It fell over her delicate shoulders with a slight curl at the bottom. Her eyes were closed, her lashes lying thick and dark against her cheeks. I needed to see into her eyes... into her heart. But she kept them shut, her face saddened by her memories.

I couldn't stop myself from reaching out to her. It seemed like an eternity since I last touched her. I skimmed my fingertips along the edge of her swollen jaw.

She gasped, but instead of pulling back, she leaned closer, her eyes fluttering open. "I know I don't deserve you," she murmured. "I wish I could do it all over..."

I slid my thumb up over her chin and then across her bottom lip. On a shaky sigh, she parted her lips. She stared directly into my eyes.

"Axel..."

I leaned down and closed the distance between my mouth and hers. My hands still cupping her face, I tipped her chin up. Then I brushed my lips gently across hers in a whisper-soft kiss.

"I'm sorry. I came here to get a story that could really make Quinn Sullivan a name people had heard of. I saw the possibility of a book deal, and I saw potential success. I came here, and I met you, for all the wrong reasons." Quinn wiped at a falling tear. "But I swear to you, that somewhere along our path, everything changed. I fell in love. I gave you my entire heart. I gave you the entirety of my soul. Not because of a book, but because I truly fell in love with you."

I nodded as the pain in my heart subsided. Quinn reached out unexpectedly and gripped her hand around my neck. In one swift movement, her mouth came down powerfully on mine, her tongue plunging past my lips as if she were claiming me, possessing me as hers. I clutched at her arms, deepening the kiss, leaving nothing but overwhelming love.

Arousal sparked in my body as if Quinn had lit me on fire. I parted her lips with the force of my tongue, my hands desperately clinging to the fabric of her shirt. Our tongues danced together as electric currents rippled through my body, my cock hardening at the sensation of Quinn's body pressing against mine, my mind spiraling out of control with the knowledge of the erotic gratification we could bring each other.

She cleared her throat. "I will apologize every day if you'll let me. Just don't walk away."

I wiped at the tears streaming down her face. "I'll never give up on us again."

The one thing that was clear was what I wanted, what I'd always wanted. I wanted her back. The only woman I'd ever truly loved. Being without her for even this short time made me realize that. The question was if I could trust her. Did I truly believe her about the book? I wondered if I deluded myself into thinking she wouldn't use me now that we were in love. That things had changed since she first arrived. Her intentions were different. Was she really in love like she claimed?

I couldn't stop believing that we had this love at first sight: crazy love. A kind of love that no matter the insecurities or the anger, never lessened. There had been a time when it would have been impossible for me to admit to myself, much less say out loud, how much I was in love. But I could clearly see that I'd fallen hard—she was all I wanted.

It hurt. It hurt badly to have Quinn lie to me. But I had to forgive in order to move on, and it did appear as if she felt truly sorry. I knew this was love. I felt it in every fiber of my being. I loved her. I always would. And I was sure that she loved me, too. But even as I thought it, doubts assailed me. This is what we needed to work out. This is what *I* needed to work out.

As we walked into the loft, I glanced around, grateful I hadn't left the place a mess. Immediately, nerves formed a tight knot in my stomach, my heartbeat slamming against my rib cage. I tossed my keys on the granite counter and immediately went to grab a bottle of red wine.

"Can I pour you a glass of wine?" I asked as I popped the cork.

"Yes, please."

At the sound of her voice, inches from my ear, I spun around to see Quinn leaning against the counter with a smile. With a thud, I dropped the bottle on the counter, grabbing her, hauling her close and covering her mouth with my own, running my hands all over Quinn's body.

With a soft moan and a light giggle, she broke away from the kiss, a frown creasing her forehead. "This is for real, right? My heart can't take it if you compare me to a groupie again," Quinn said, her voice cracking slightly.

I shook my head, continuing to run my hands over her back. "I shouldn't have said those things, or acted that way. I was mean and wrong. I was hurt, but that doesn't excuse me lashing out at you." I stopped, shaking my head, closing my eyes briefly. "I know I hurt you, too."

"I thought I lost you," she said, looking away briefly.

"I don't want our love to be *delicate* like you said. We're strong enough to get through anything. Even if I did a horrible job of showing you that." My heartbeat harsh in my chest, I looked into Quinn's eyes. "Do you forgive me?" I asked, my eyes searching hers.

I saw regret cloud her eyes before she turned away. I felt everything in my body freeze as I gazed at the woman I loved, attempting to read the emotions in her eyes, trying to determine their meaning.

With tears releasing from her eyes, Quinn placed a hand on my arm. "Axel, please don't apologize—

" She broke off, swallowing hard. "I'll never doubt your love for me... for us. I'll always trust in you... as long as you can trust in me." She stopped, wiping at her tears. "I love you. I always will."

Any other words were forgotten as I brought our mouths together.

Quinn laughed around the kisses as I led her to the room and kicked the door to the bedroom open, bundled her in my arms, and with long strides, placed Quinn down onto the bed.

"I want you," I said. With a groan, I rapidly began to undress her, only to be rewarded with Quinn doing the same to me.

"God, I want you, too," she said, her voice breathless, as she frantically pulled at my pants.

I felt my body burn in eager anticipation as I stared down at the vision of Quinn splayed out in front of me. I ran a finger down the line of her throat, down the midline of her body, before stopping at the juncture of her thighs.

Locking my eyes on hers, I stroked a finger deep inside her, her walls clamping tight against my invasion. With a groan, I withdrew, my finger covered with Quinn's sexual desire.

I loved how good it was between us. She was always so responsive to my touch. I closed my eyes briefly, my desire growing thicker.

"I've missed this," I said with a groan, fighting the urge to spread Quinn's legs and press my cock deep inside her willing warmth.

But I wanted to take my time. Separating her pussy lips, I watched in heated fascination as she lost control. With every drag and pull of my finger, Quinn's walls clenched and released in rhythmic pulses, her cream easing down and covering my hand. All control was lost.

"I've got to taste you," I said, spreading her legs farther apart.

I tasted.

I devoured.

She was mine again.

* * * * *

Quinn

The first stroke of Axel's tongue against me had me rearing my body up and off the mattress, a cry tumbling from my lips. I moaned softly, my hands coming out to brace myself on the bed as Axel flicked his tongue over and around my clit, toying with me before surrounding my pleasure point completely within the warm cavern of his mouth.

On and on it went, alternating between stabbing flicks of his tongue and long sweeping kisses, driving my passion to a whole new level. When Axel drew his tongue completely out and nibbled gently, an orgasm washed over me—gentle at first but then intense as it grew. His fingers slid into me, going deep, causing stars to flash behind my tightly closed lids as I came, crying out as the tremors rocked my entire body. Entirely wrung out, my body collapsed onto the mattress, my muscles weak

"I'm not done with you yet," Axel promised, his voice dark, as he began to sink into me. But before pressing inside me fully, he paused, his breath coming out coarsely. "Tell me you love me, Quinn. That you've never stopped."

I moaned, grinding my body against his, my face flushed with hunger. "I—I love you, Axel," I cried when he inched farther inside me.

He pressed his hand between us, finding my clit and working it as he delivered small, shallow thrusts. "Tell me you want me," he demanded.

"I want you!"

At my admission, Axel slid all the way in. Grasping my ass, he lifted me and began to thrust. His fingers dug into my hips as he held onto me, alternating the thrusts between long and deep, and shallow and quick, angling my body along his for our mutual pleasure.

I wrapped my legs around Axel's waist, digging my heels into his back. "Faster," I panted as his fingers scored deep into the globes of my bottom, his head thrown back, eyes shut.

Soon our mutual groans echoed in the room, bouncing off the walls as his strokes became softer, easier, eventually subsiding.

Sweat poured off our bodies. I opened my eyes and released a sigh, the afterglow of perfect lovemaking seeming to wash away any hurt of the past.

I felt Axel's hand feather across my breasts, and I smiled. "That was really nice," I said, hissing slightly when Axel's thumb ran over my overly sensitive nipple.

Axel laughed, a thoroughly perfect sound.

"I have something to ask you," he said, as he grabbed a piece of my hair and played with it between his fingers. "Did you really mean it when you said you were planning on staying in LA?"

"Yes. I can't imagine my life without you. I decided—"

My words were cut off when Axel surprised me by covering my mouth with his. I succumbed instantly to the touch. Slowly, he drew away from me.

He placed his hands on either side of my face. "I can't imagine my life without you, either."

Quinn

The apartment was shrouded in darkness when I finally awoke from the best sleep I had had in days. Eyes still adjusting to the lack of light, I peered at the digital alarm clock on Axel's nightstand and was surprised to discover that it was almost three o'clock in the morning. The events of the past days had thoroughly worn me out. Sighing in contentment, I stretched my arms out above my head, still relishing the afterglow of the most amazing sex. The tension that had weighed me down had all but disappeared, replaced by a sense of serenity.

Moving to get up from the bed, I realized Axel was nowhere to be found. I quickly padded out of the room toward the kitchen. Passing by the bathroom, the sound of running water grabbed my attention. Pushing open the door, I smiled at the sight of a very naked, and extremely handsome man drawing a bath.

"Axel?" I asked curiously, stepping further into the room. His head whipped around at the sound of my voice, and my heart melted when Axel smiled at me sensually.

"You're not supposed to be awake yet," he admonished me playfully, moving away from the claw-foot bathtub as he came to stand in front of me. "I wanted to let you get a bit more sleep before I woke you up for your surprise."

"My surprise?" I asked in confusion, looking past him at the rose petals floating atop the water's surface. He had lined up bath oils and salts along the bathroom sink. He had a terrycloth robe folded neatly on top of the vanity and a glass of red wine sitting beside it. I glanced up at him in confusion. "What is all this?"

"We're celebrating a very special day today," he said, as he reached out to tuck a wayward strand of hair behind my ear.

"Axel…" I sighed. I didn't deserve all this. Not after the way I had treated him. I should be doing all the romantic gestures. "What day are we celebrating?"

"The day you moved into my home," Axel whispered, cupping my face in his hands as he leaned forward and placed a gentle kiss on my lips. When we parted, his hands traveled down my sides until both palms rested against my nude bottom.

"What?" I squeaked, my voice catching in my throat as I pressed my naked body against his. "Did you just say—"

"Shhh," Axel silenced me, smiling as he kissed me gently again. "Just relax and enjoy your bath while the water's still hot. We'll talk later, okay?"

"Okay," I agreed, offering him a reassuring smile as he moved past me and turned to leave the room.

"Enjoy the bath," he said with a smile, stepping out into the dimly lit hallway and closing the door behind him.

Sighing in contentment, I carefully lowered myself into the tub. I hissed as the hot water enveloped my skin. Closing my eyes, I tried not to overthink the comment Axel had just made. It was almost cruel that I had to wait and see what he meant by that. Did he really want me to move in?

I stepped out of the bathroom twenty minutes later, dressed in Axel's soft robe. My stomach growled as I entered the kitchen and my nose was immediately assaulted by the sight of freshly sliced strawberries and the delicious aroma of freshly brewed coffee.

"You look beautiful," Axel commented, pulling out a chair and helping me take a seat in front of the lavishly decorated table. I giggled at how easily he could just walk around naked. He still hadn't put a stitch of clothing on.

"I can't believe you're doing all this. It's too much."

"I told you that we're celebrating a special day," he insisted, leaning over the back of my chair to whisper in my ear. "This is the day you agree to move in with me." His warm breath tickled my skin, causing a shiver to course through my body. I turned my head to face him, searching his eyes for clarity.

"I'd love to," I whispered, reaching out to stroke Axel's cheek.

"I don't want to spend another night apart," he said in a low voice, pressing his face into the palm of my hand as we gazed at each other with love in our eyes.

We stayed like that for a while, both of us absorbing what we had just agreed to while trying to get a handle on our emotions. I brought Axel's hand up to my lips, placing a gentle kiss as I offered him a warm smile.

"I thought I lost you," I said softly, fighting back the tears. "This is like a dream. I have you back."

"My heart has always been with you. But, Quinn," Axel said, grabbing my chin in his hand and forcing me to meet his gaze. "No more secrets.

You can tell me anything. You don't hold back anything anymore."

"I promise," I agreed, nodding my head with conviction. Leaning forward, he placed a gentle kiss against my lips. "I love you," I declared, wrapping my arms around Axel's waist.

"And I'll always love you," Axel promised me sincerely, burying his face into my hair as I laid my head down against his chest. "And I swear to you that things are going to be different from now on. You and I together, forever."

"I like the sound of that," I whispered, snuggling closer in Axel's hold.

He lifted me out of the chair and pulled me closer into his embrace. I wrapped my arms around his neck, holding onto him as tightly as I would forever hold onto our love: a love that was anything but delicate and scarred.

I suddenly needed Axel like I'd never needed him before. It didn't help that he stood naked tempting me with his every move. I wanted intimacy, connection, and love. I wanted to please him once again completely.

Without saying a single word, I kissed my way down his toned chest until I reached his large, erect cock. I stopped to stare at his manhood, never before finding a man as enticing. I pressed my lips to the tip of his cock, and gradually worked my tongue to the base. I picked up the pace, moving up and down while squeezing tight with my hand. I moaned as I scraped my teeth along the sides of his tightening cock. I moved my hand to his balls and began to sensually massage. He pumped his cock deeper and began to fuck my mouth with fury, removing all traces of sensuality. He grabbed me by the hair and raised my head up and down, driving towards orgasm. Suddenly he stopped and tried to pull away.

I shook my head and murmured, "No, I want to taste you," and continued to suck up and down his entire shaft.

He moaned loudly. "Oh god, Quinn, I'm going to come!"

I tightened my lips and moved my tongue with a quickened speed, driving him to climax with every flick of my tongue. I wanted him. I wanted his release. I could hear his breathing catch and felt his balls tighten beneath my massaging fingers. He drove his cock as deep as my mouth could take and released his hot seed in the back of my throat as he cried out my name.

He lifted me abruptly and turned me on to my stomach on the kitchen floor. He lowered his hard body on top of mine and began to kiss and nibble the back of my neck.

"You're amazing." He lowered his hand to the crease of my bottom and seductively stroked. "I want you here." Axel stood, pulled me up and then lifted me in his arms.

"What about breakfast?"

"It can wait; I can't," he said, not even pausing as he carried me back to the bedroom, setting me gently on the bed and then went into the bathroom, returning with a bottle of lubricant and a phallus made of glass.

My heart fluttered and my sex clenched. I felt nervous but highly aroused. I had been waiting for this day, and now seemed so right. I wanted to please him in every single way possible. Axel applied some lubricant to my anus and pressed his finger past the entrance to lubricate further. He pumped his finger in and out and then added a second finger. I struggled for breath as he spread his fingers apart so he could stretch me further.

I panted and moaned with every movement. I pressed my ass to his fingers, desperate for more. Being on the edge of climax drove me crazy with lust. Axel removed his fingers, leaving me with an empty void. I could hear him placing lubrication on his cock and my mouth watered at the thought of him taking me in the most intimate of places.

"I want you where no one else has been. I want you completely," Axel gruffly said as he pressed his cock against my waiting entrance.

Very slowly, Axel moved his cock past my now slick and ready opening. Kissing my neck softly, he whispered his love to me as he pressed deeper. I had never felt something so intimate, so erotic, and so passionate. He continued on, spreading my tender hole. I whimpered as I felt the pain of his possession and instantly panicked. I suddenly wasn't sure if I was ready.

Axel paused so I could get accustomed to the feel. "Just relax, Quinn. You're doing so well. I promise that you're ready. I made sure you would be able to take me. You feel so tight, so hot. Press into me," he coaxed.

I pressed back as he directed and allowed his hardness to push in further. The intensity overwhelmed me, and Axel only added to it when he reached around and found my clit with his fingers. He rolled his finger around my swollen desire as he drove even deeper. I moaned in pleasure, as well as pain, and suddenly allowed the climax to take over. I bucked against him, driving him all the way into the depths of my body. I screamed as orgasmic pulses rushed through my forbidden channel.

Axel continued to pump in and out. Suddenly I felt something else. I shuddered as the cold glass dildo slid into my pussy. The toy quickly warmed within the heat of my body. It was an incredible feeling as he thrust it in and out of my vagina as he continued to fuck my ass. Every thrust drove me higher. I felt so full, so possessed. I cried out his name as his cock and the toy moved in and out at a relentless pace. Wave after wave of incredible bliss rolled over me like a tsunami.

"Axel!" I moaned.

"Take all of me. You're mine, Quinn. Mine," Axel growled.

Axel continued to press on harder and harder as I pleaded for more. All gentleness and slow easing was replaced with fever and crazed desire. He grabbed both sides of my ass and drove deeper. I loved the submissive feel. I loved being overcome in such a primal way. Axel sunk his hardness deeper than I thought possible and came as his body shook in completion. He moved his cock in and out a few more times in slow, sensual strokes. He then pulled out and rolled onto his back to catch his breath.

I remained on my stomach, unable to move, gasping for air. Axel rubbed his hand up and down my back while I recovered from the most amazing sexual event of my life. Never could I have imagined something so powerful, so erotic. This was like no other sex. I felt closer to Axel than I ever had before. I was his, and I wanted nothing more.

Finally, he broke the blissful silence first. "Are you all right? I didn't hurt you, did I?"

"Oh, I'm better than all right. I never knew it would be like that."

"Are you sure? I was harder than I wanted to be. I lost control," Axel said with worry in his voice.

I simply smiled.

He brushed some of the loose hair away from my face. "You're everything." He paused, and then kissed me on the forehead. "You are mine."

I silently nodded in response.

Chapter 17

Goodbye To The Dark

Quinn

I woke up to the sound of Axel in the shower. I looked at the disheveled bed and smiled with the memory of the night before. It seemed like every time Axel and I had sex, it was better than the last. I would think I had the best sex of my life, only to feel that way the next time. "Absolutely amazing" would be an understatement. He was so attentive, so loving, and he demanded in bed in a way that only Axel could do. God, I loved this man.

The water stopped, and shortly after the bathroom door opened. Axel had a towel wrapped around his waist. His muscular chest looked mouthwatering with the drops of water dripping down to his perfect abs. He looked happy with a huge Cheshire grin. He leaned against the doorframe and just gazed at me.

"You're gorgeous. You make me so happy, seeing you lying in my bed." He made his way to the edge of the bed and bent down to place a kiss on my forehead. "Get up and get showered. I have a surprise today."

"A surprise, what?"

"Get up and get ready and you'll see," he answered. He softly ran his fingers through my hair before simply stating, "I love you."

I tried to get ready as quickly as I could. I absolutely loved surprises. Obviously, he had something in mind to do today. The weather was lovely outside, so I was able to put on a nice summer dress. Axel loved when I wore dresses, stating it was because he had easier access. I smiled to myself, remembering how I had been nervous that I didn't look "cool" or "hip" enough for him. I loved how Axel loved me for me. I gazed at my reflection in the mirror and felt pretty. Axel had a way of making me feel beautiful. Ever since being with him, my self-esteem had grown by leaps and bounds. He did wonders for my ego. He allowed me to feel confident about my womanly curves, comfortable with my natural beauty. Every part of my body now seemed sensual and desirable. I was a confident and elegant woman.

I walked into the kitchen to find Axel finishing up the last details of the breakfast we had left unfinished only hours before. He had made a fruit salad and strawberry scones. He had already set the table complete with red roses in a vase in the center. The sliding glass door was open, letting in the warm, fresh air, and I could hear the birds chirping outside. Everything seemed so romantic, so special, like a love story.

"My, my, I never knew you could be so romantic. A girl could get used to this type of treatment," I lovingly teased as I walked over to kiss him on the cheek.

"You deserve nothing but the best." He took a step back so he could take a full look at me. "You are the most beautiful woman I've ever had the pleasure of laying eyes on. Look at you! I've never been so blown away by someone as I am with you."

I blushed and made my way to the table. Axel followed with the rest of breakfast and sat across from me. He raised a champagne glass filled with mimosa and silently toasted.

I took a bite of the scone. "Mmmm, this is good! You're quite the baker."

Axel laughed before he admitted, "It's from a box."

"Well, I like it anyway. Thank you for going through so much effort. I love you for it."

"I love you, too, Quinn Sullivan." He said my name with a huge smile on his face. He had such a boyish charm when he wanted to.

We sat and ate in silence for a while, just enjoying being in each other's presence and taking in the wonderful morning. The breakfast, the morning, and the man were perfect.

Axel finally stood up and lifted me out of my chair and hugged me tight to his chest. "I'm so lucky to have you." He lifted my chin so I looked into his eyes. "Get your shoes on, sweetheart. I have something to show you. Your surprise."

The whole way in the car I kept pestering Axel to tell me where we were going. He would simply smile and lightly pat my knee, not giving in to the onslaught of questions. We drove for quite some time along a beautiful curving road. The trees leaned over them from all sides. They created a tunnel, with the clear blue sky peeking between the leaves. I stared into the dense forest, taking the time to reflect. The past few weeks had been a whirlwind of love and passion, but also scarred with intense darkness.

Lost in such deep thought, it took me a moment to realize Axel had pulled over onto the side of the road. I turned to him, about to ask why he stopped, when I saw that he was staring straight ahead. His jovial mood was replaced with seriousness. I followed his gaze to a two-story wooden cabin overlooking a cliff.

I stared out into the canyon below and took in the beauty. The view from where the cabin stood was magnificent. There was something magical about the setting behind the house. The trees looked so full of life. The small creek far below glistened, and the expanse of open air seemed all-powerful.

"Who lives here? Who are we visiting?" I asked in confusion.

"I'm not telling you yet. It's a surprise," Axel teased as he got out of the car and walked around to open my door.

Axel reached for my hand and led me to the front porch without saying another word. When he reached the front door, he reached into his pocket and pulled out a key. Instead of knocking, he inserted the key and opened the door. Before I could protest, he softly pulled me inside. I looked around cautiously and noticed the cabin was completely empty.

I looked around again at the empty house and asked, "Why are we in a vacant cabin in the middle of nowhere?"

Axel smiled and took both of my hands into his. "It's ours. I bought it so we could have a place that is one hundred percent ours. Not my loft, but a brand new house—a home, our home—filled with only our memories."

Speechless, I just stood in place, stunned with the realization that I was inside our new home.

"I hope you like it. I promise the only decision I make is the house, but you can decorate it however you choose. You can do whatever you want to make it ours. Do you like it?" Axel asked nervously.

I wrapped my arms around Axel's neck and looked into his eyes. "I love it! I love you! I love everything!"

"Come on, let me show you around," Axel said as he grabbed me by the hand to lead me through the house.

He began by showing me all of the rooms. He walked into one room in particular, stopped, and faced me with a smile.

"I was thinking about this room for your office. It has the best view of the canyon," Axel suggested with a huge grin.

I opened my mouth in shock. "What? My office? What do I need an office for?"

"You'll need a quiet place to concentrate while you work on your book. Really explaining my life won't be an easy task," Axel explained.

"I told you I wasn't going to write the book."

"And I'm telling you to. Your grandmother was right. Quinn Sullivan is too special of a name not to see it in print. And I think a biography may be a great way of closure for me. A way for me to walk away and never look back. My drug dealing days are over. I don't want to walk back into another club for as long as I live. I want you to write my story."

"Oh, Axel. Are you sure?"

"Yes. No more drugs. No more partying. No more nightlife. Those days are over. We start over completely."

I nodded. "I agree. Let's start over. Let's say goodbye to the dark."

He laughed and a twinkle lit up his eye. "No more vampire hours."

"No more vampire hours," I agreed.

"It might not be easy breaking away."

"But we will figure it out together."

He grabbed my hand and softly pulled me into an embrace. I could hear his heart beat against his chest. We stayed like that for a while. We took the time to just let everything sink in.

He turned me gently so I faced him. He lowered his lips, softly pressing them to mine. He pulled away and stared deep into my eyes.

"I love you. I love you more than I imagined possible. When I'm with you, I feel a love stronger than I thought could exist. I finally found what I longed for. I found you," Axel passionately declared.

He stared at me for a few moments and then lowered himself onto one knee. He pulled a ring box from his pocket and placed the ring onto my finger in one fluid motion, I barely knew what was happening.

"Quinn Sullivan, I love you more than anything, and I can't imagine not having you in my life. Will you marry me?"

I stood in disbelief for a few moments as I looked into Axel's eyes. He remained kneeling, awaiting my answer. "Yes! Of course I'll marry you! Oh, Axel, I love you so much!"

He stood up and placed the most passionate kiss of my life on my lips. His tongue danced with mine, and our breaths intertwined. He held me so tight and with so much emotion, I could hardly breathe.

"I swear I'll make you happy. I swear I'll make you the happiest wife there is," he promised.

I pulled away so I could admire the ring. It was gorgeous! A pink diamond with rubies circling the stone. "Axel, the ring is so pretty, and so feminine. You really didn't need to—"

Axel interrupted. "I want there to be no question in anyone's mind that you are taken. You are mine!"

"Yes, yes! I'm yours, forever. I promise I'll be the best wife I can. I promise I'll do everything to make you happy." I paused to regain my composure. "Thank you for taking me here. It means the world that you would give us a home to call our own." I looked at Axel through my tear-filled eyes. "Thank you for believing in me, and believing in us."

Axel held me close. "I'm finally done searching. I found the light in all the fucked up darkness my life once was…I found you… Quinn Sullivan."

The End

Alta Hensley is a USA TODAY bestselling erotic romance author who has had #1 top-selling books in dark, contemporary, BDSM, erotic science fiction, humor, suspense and historical. She writes the hot, dark, and dirty romance.

Being a multi-published author in the romance genre, Alta is known for her dark, gritty alpha heroes, sometimes sweet love stories, hot eroticism, and engaging tales of the constant struggle between dominance and submission.

Facebook:
https://www.facebook.com/AltaHensleyAuthor/

Amazon: http://amzn.to/2e4R1ii

Twitter: https://twitter.com/AltaHensley

Website: www.altahensley.com

Join her mailing list:

http://www.subscribepage.com/i0n8g9

Titles by Alta Hensley

Mama's Boy (April 2017)

Like Poison-Vagabond Series #1 (May 2017)

Bad, Bad, Girl- Complete Traditional Love Series (March 28, 2017)

Little Victorian Ladies Anthology (February 22, 2017)

No White Knight

Dark Feather

Caring For Citrine

Traditional Love

Traditional Terms

Traditional Change

Poppa's Progeny

In the Palace of Lazar - Harem (Book One)

Conquering Lazar - Harem (Book Two)

The Slave Huntsman

The Dark Forest

Captured by Time (with Carolyn Faulkner)

A New Forever (with Carolyn Faulkner)

Enrolling Little Etta (with Allison West)

The Nanny (with Allison West)

Little Secrets (with Allison West)

Maddox, The Black Stallion Trilogy #1 (with Maggie Ryan)

Stryder, The Black Stallion Trilogy #2 (with Maggie Ryan)

Anson, The Black Stallion Trilogy #3 (with Maggie Ryan)

42198455R00204

Made in the USA
Middletown, DE
06 April 2017